The Buried Knight

Book One

The Innisfail Cycle

Angela Laverghetta

admitted once it was likely arson and that some people still believed we were in league with the devil.

Our family legacy of weirdness runs long and deep.

Going to college for four years in Southern Nevada had been a respite from condemnation, but I'd missed my grandparents too much to stay two more years to finish my master's in museum curating. I came back to Carson and got an internship at the Nevada State Museum. A one-year break became two as Grandpa got sick and I felt the need to stay longer to help.

My grandmother, who loved "working the numbers" as she liked to say, ran the business side of the retirement home almost until the day she passed. It's been a little over a year since they both died within weeks of each other. I was told a few times at the funeral it's common for longtime partners as if that would make the pain less. It didn't. They were my only family, my best friends, and my safe harbor.

My internship, carting the residents back and forth to their appointments in the van, and now the day-to-day business of the retirement home kept me too busy during the day to wallow in grief.

Nights were another matter.

Honestly, after an entire year I still hadn't decided what I was going to do about the retirement home. Their will gave three options: sell it, run it, or hire someone to run it. Unlike Grandma, I didn't like the numbers at all, or more accurately they didn't like me. I really needed to at least hire an administrative assistant, but the whole hiring process seemed even more daunting than math.

I really didn't want to sell it. It was my only connection to my family. I was the only Wylde left. My mom didn't count. She left me when I was five and I haven't seen her since. Not even a snail mail letter. As for my dad? Who knows. When I used to ask as a child, Grandpa assured me I was good Wylde stock so it didn't matter. I pretended to agree, but of course it mattered. I hated not knowing.

This is why, before they'd passed, I'd kept secret the search for my parents.

Just like the Brownie in my bedroom.

I stepped in and used my hip to close the door, giving it an extra bump to get the wood past the old doorframe. It's barely large enough to be called a bedroom. I believe it used to be a back porch that was walled in back in the '80s. Only a metal framed single bed pushed into the upper left corner below the one small window and a desk, dresser, and armoire, fighting for space on the opposite wall, were able to fit. A very tight fit. Which was why Grandpa had to build a high shelf that ran along the entire perimeter to hold what started as one brass cocker spaniel he'd purchased for me from an antique shop in Virginia City and was now a zoo of brass fauna cultivated over years of antiquing.

"Nibbleink," I called. "You have three seconds to come out or I'm cutting off your clothes allowance."

My words were met with silence.

"One... "

Silence.

"Two...

"Two and a half...

"Two and three quarters... " I heard a rustle from under the bed. A doll-sized white cowboy hat sitting between long ragged ears crawled out of the shadows followed by a spindly, stick-like body in a lurid pink ballgown from last year's Barbie at the Ball Collection. She — I'm still not quite sure if that gender is accurate, but it's my best guess and she hasn't corrected me — stood up her full eleven-ish inches and used her long needle-like fingers to reposition the hat. Then she attempted to smooth out the wrinkles in her dress. The Brownie, because that's what she told me she was, straightened and looked up at me with shiny black eyes that took up most of her face.

"Would you have anything to do with the state of Ms. Carlton and the other residents this morning?" I asked.

Nibbleink huffed. "Ms. Carlton was sad." She crossed her arms and glared. "She always leaves me a cookie, so I made her happy."

I had a feeling Ms. Carlton wasn't leaving out the cookie for Nibs. The old woman had dementia and often thought her partner Ms. Kelly was still alive. She probably left the cookie for her.

"And the others?"

Nibbleink shrugged. "They don't give me cookies. I made them not happy."

I drew in a deep breath and let it out slowly. "How long will this happy — not happy last?"

"Not long."

"In human time."

Nibbleink lifted one of her crossed arms and tapped a long finger against her lipless mouth. "Two days."

I rubbed a hand over my face trying not to yell. "Nibs, we talked about this last spring. Never again or you'll *never* get another stitch of clothing, I mean it."

The Brownie threw her hands in the air. She turned around, mumbling to herself, and crouched to hide back under the bed.

"Wait, Nibs," I called to her. "Can I ask you a question?" There was something I didn't quite understand about our relationship. Honestly, there were a lot of things I didn't understand, but this question was relevant to the situation.

The Brownie turned and crossed her arms, again. "Do I get sugar?"

I reached into my oversized purse sitting on the dresser and pulled out a granola bar. "It's all I have right now."

Nibs reached out for the bar and I dropped it into her hands. She ripped into the packaging with her pointed teeth and said "ask question" around a large bite of oats and chocolate chips.

"Not that I'm complaining, but why haven't you ever put your Brownie whammy on me? Just curious and it's *not* an invitation."

Nibs looked insulted. "Duty before friendship."

"I'm a duty?" This information was new. "What does that mean?"

Nibs rolled her eyes and shook her head at me in pity. She popped the rest of the bar in her mouth, the ends sticking out on either side, and scurried back under the bed. Conversation over.

I sighed. About a year ago, I'd found Nibbleink cowering under a lifted truck parked on Carson Street. Normally, I would have walked on by and pretended I couldn't see her. It's easier to just ignore the things I can see but no one else can. Easier for me and easier for the people around me. But she'd been bleeding and I couldn't bring myself to leave her there, whimpering and crying large crocodile tears. I'd taken her home to clean and bandage her wound. After which, the little Brownie just kept coming up with new ailments to justify staying longer and before I knew it, I was buying doll clothes off the Internet to feed her fashion addiction.

I did get something out of the relationship, besides credit card debt and a foot-tall kid sister the universe decided I needed. I'd learned more about the fae from Nibs than I'd ever learned on my own. Okay, I'd learned almost *everything* I knew about the fae from Nibs, even if she only gives information in her own time and in her own way. And each time she tells me or shows me something new the more I realize how much I still don't know. I'm worried it's going to get me in real trouble one of these days.

There is one question, though, Nibs has not answered for me. Why me? Why does being a Wylde mean I'm cursed? She won't or can't tell me the reason I can see what I like to call "the weird and bizarre otherworld of nonstop danger and stress" or the "Otherworld" for short. The world that has plagued my family for generations. The world that no matter how hard I try to ignore, always seems to find me.

Not for the first time, I've wondered if my mom had stuck around she would have been helpful. If nothing else, she could have had the decency to tell me who my father was. On my birth certificate, it says "unknown" where my father's name should be. I didn't even know you could say that on a government document. I tried to find the Record of Live Birth from the hospital, but it's mysteriously missing. Sometimes, I find myself scrutinizing the local middle-aged men to see if we have similar features. This, of course, only adds to my weird girl persona.

Carson City is not as small as say Montpelier, Vermont — the smallest state capitol — we're not even in the bottom ten smallest—I looked it up—but the truth is, everyone knows everyone here, and everyone knows the "weird Wylde family." I've tried my whole life to hide the fact I see things no one else can, but I haven't always been successful. Nibbleink being one of the times my desire to help won out over self-preservation. I could move, but every time I've considered it, I find something to talk myself out of it. Taking over the retirement home is only the most recent reason to stay.

I checked my phone for any appointments the residents had that I would have to reschedule due to our second fae-related Woodstock. There was only one and I was able to change the date and time online. I then swapped jammies and narwhal slippers for slacks and a long-sleeved knit shirt. With nothing more to do, and a desperate need to leave the crazy at home, I decided to head to the museum and start my other job early. No pay, but hours of tours, paperwork, and dust? Heaven.

Chapter Two

As I followed my usual route to the museum, I couldn't rid myself of the guilt of leaving the retirement home in chaos. I trusted Everett and the staff. I didn't trust Nibs. The concrete sidewalk felt glacial beneath my feet and an early storm a day ago had laid a dusting of snow on the hills in the distance. Winter would be here soon, but not yet. For now, the intense desert sun would conquer the cold during the day. I could already feel its warmth as it rose higher in the East.

My walk up Curry Street took me past many small businesses all nestled in historic houses and colored like well-dressed Victorian ladies. Carson City was a cozy mix of small town and tourist trap. Grandpa and I used to visit the numerous antique shops at least once a month. Even if I couldn't get him to talk about why we Wyldes were cursed, I could at least get him to talk about local history.

Perfect, now I was worried about leaving the home in crisis *and* sad about Grandpa.

Maybe a cup of tea would help soothe my nerves.

Tea-Lightful, a coffee and tea shop, was one I'd frequented in the past and seemed mostly fae free. I took the three steps to the front porch and opened the creaking old screen door, nearly running over Sam Lehrman, Carson's premier lawyer — just ask his billboards. I mumbled an apology and sidled out of his way. He didn't notice. Good. I'd take being ignored over outright disdain any day of the week. But looking in his direction meant I missed that there was someone else in the way.

I bumped into them and spun around, my mouth open to apologize. The fae stood in line to order covered from pointy ears to clawed toes in sable fur, and not the kind you find in your grandmother's old clothes trunk. Their dark marble eyes peered at me from above the phone they held in their paw. Waiting.

With no time to school my response, my eyes widened, and I only got out the 's' in sorry, the rest caught in my throat. A middle-aged guy wearing socks and sandals in front of the fae glanced back at me with an odd look. Tea was not worth the consternation. I turned and rushed out the door.

It's really not too hard to see why people in this city think I'm weird. The fae had been glamoured. It's a catch-all term for fae magic. Nibs taught me. It can either hide a fae completely from normal humans or change what the human sees, creating a different more acceptable exterior. But it doesn't work on me. I can always see what's hidden, so I have to pretend I don't and that sucks. From everyone else's perspective in the tea shop, I'd hissed and then run away from a perfectly normal-looking college student. I was the looney.

Sans tea, I made it to the museum. I waved to Kevin at the front desk and took the stairs to the first floor of the museum's Calhoun wing. I reached the top and paused. A guy in all in black, crouched near the glass case of the new traveling exhibit "Medieval Weaponry."

A ghost? As if seeing the fae wasn't bad enough, I can see the recently departed, too. Got to love a curse with layers. Nibs doesn't know much about ghosts or even why I see them, but from what she knows, ghosts are attached to items or places. There are a few well-known haunted houses in the historical district and the ghost tours love to point them out. But a few of the items in the museum are haunted as well. According to Nibs, for a ghost to exist there needs to be a bit of magic and a dash of tragedy.

But the guy looked like he was tampering with a lock. Ghosts couldn't become corporeal enough to manage that.

"Hey! There's an alarm, you know!" My indignation over someone potentially harming an exhibit overrode my usual stranger anxiety.

He jerked backward, teetering a moment. I thought he might topple, but he steadied and looked over his shoulder with eyebrows raised high enough to nearly touch his black beanie. His hazel eyes leaned toward golden and almost matched the hair that had escaped and curled along the bottom of the beanie. I followed the angle of his high cheekbones to his bold nose and down to full lips. If I'd planned on saying anything else, the words disappeared. I just stared. I'd never seen anyone so attractive in real life.

Slowly, he stood. Now I could see the rest of him, not overly tall with wide shoulders and a tapered waist, covered in shades of black from the black beanie to a long, dark coat over a turtleneck with tactical pants tucked into heavy boots and even leather gloves. What did this guy do, watch a tv show to get thief wardrobe ideas?

Thief! Right. I needed to handle the situation and not just gawk.

I opened my mouth to call down the stairs to Kevin. I paused with my mouth open like one of the stuffed fish over in Natural History. Wait. Take a moment. I needed to think this through. He'd seemed startled when I had spoken to him. As if he'd thought no one would notice him even though he was out in the open. Before I brought in reinforcements and created a huge incident, I needed to know if he was noticeable *only* to me. I'd made that horrible mistake one too many times in my life.

"How did you... I mean do you know... How did you get in?

Into the museum?" I clenched my fists at my sides, willing myself to look him in the eyes as my heart raced in my chest. The question needed to be asked. If he didn't know how he got to the museum, he could be a ghost, just more solid than I'm used to seeing them. Even if he didn't have the superimposed image I normally noticed with glamour, there was the other possibility he was fae.

When he didn't answer right away, I managed to force out, "Are you fae?"

One moment I was looking at him from across the room and the next he stood a few inches from me. His face hovered over mine and he canted his head slightly in scrutiny. He was close enough I could make out the bright flecks of color in his eyes and how his olive-tinged skin appeared nearly poreless.

My brain screamed he was too close. Way too close. My whole body tightened at once. My chest felt empty of all air. Barely suppressing a squeak, I sidestepped from under his looming frame and took a deep shuddering breath.

The thief's eyes widened and he raised a gloved hand as if calming a frightened animal and took an additional step back. I might have taken offense, but I enjoyed the return of my personal space and the ability to breathe.

"You can see me." His eyes surveyed me from head to toe. "This is unexpected." There was an accent. English? Scottish? I couldn't place it.

"I hate to tell you, but the outfit doesn't make you invisible," I managed to say without stumbling, gesturing up and down to reference the whole how-to-be-a-thief package.

"No, but my glamour should have," he said sharply.

Not a ghost then. Maybe he was using a type of glamour I was unfamiliar with. Honestly, my knowledge of the fae was so limited, he could easily be something I'd never seen before.

"What were you... over there... what were you trying to steal?" I pointed past him to the glass case he'd been near holding three swords on stepped glass shelves. What would a fae want with them? The swords were special because they were in great shape for their age and mostly intact, not because they were magical. At least I didn't think so. They were on loan from a collector in the area. A very rich, very esteemed business owner who had a penchant for very old, very awesome medieval swords, and the substantial pocketbook to purchase them.

The thief glared. "Retrieving what is mine is not stealing."

"They were purchased legally," I defended, my indignation helping me speak clearly. I didn't like the implication the museum would display stolen goods. Well, recently stolen goods anyway.

"I don't have time for this." He turned back toward the swords in the case, his whole demeanor dismissive.

"But those swords are over a thousand years old. How could any of them possibly be yours?" How old could the fae live? Nothing like another reminder of how little I really knew.

"The one in the middle. It was found in a tomb, correct?" the thief asked, ignoring my ownership question.

"Yes. From somewhere in the UK." I wasn't very familiar with the specifics. Medieval weapons weren't my focus of study.

Heels echoed from the foyer and headed in our direction. I looked toward the stairs. Diana Wovoka, one of the museum curators and my boss, walked up them. She stared down at her phone screen while expertly balancing a coffee and still using her thumb to type.

I looked back toward the thief and found the room empty. I couldn't see him in any direction. He was just gone. Great, what if he was off trying to steal other artifacts?

Diana glanced up from her phone as she neared and paused. "Genny, everything alright?"

"Oh yeah, I needed... the bathrooms in the North building, you know with the construction, so I had to use these ones." Distracted, my words tumbled out, barely coherent. How could that thief have disappeared so quickly? The display cases were glass; it wasn't like he'd be able to hide behind them.

"I swear we live in a constant state of construction around here," Diana said with a sigh. She took a sip of her coffee. "How are you holding up at home?"

I shrugged. "I really need to hire an office manager or at least an assistant. Why is QuickBooks so fussy?"

"Don't ask me. That's why I have an accountant. You know you can take some time off. Your internship isn't going anywhere."

"You've said and I appreciate it, I do, but if I stay at the home it's just a reminder that they're gone." I forced myself to concentrate on Diana and not the well of depression lurking and waiting to pounce.

"All right then would you be able to come in early tomorrow? I've got a donation from a local estate that needs to be catalogued. I could use the extra help. Drinks on me at the Old Globe Saloon after." Diana would very much like us to be friends as well as coworkers. Maybe because she grew up on the Pyramid Lake Reservation and had no prior knowledge of me before I started working at the museum, but she thinks I'm fun to be around. I'll admit, it was nice to be just plain Genny Wylde. Almost as freeing as my first year of college when no one knew me. It didn't last, of course. Respond to a ghost you thought was just a coed one too many times and you tend to develop a reputation. Fast.

"Yes, of course." I tried not to squeal with eagerness over cataloging. Helping with local artifacts was literally my favorite part of the job. I'm convinced if I search deep enough something will turn up that might explain why I can see the things I see. If I had to suffer with pretending not to see the fae, ghosts, and nightmare-causing monsters it would be nice to know why.

A notification chimed from Diana's phone and she glanced at it with a sigh. "More on those poor mustangs. Can you believe it's happened again?" When I didn't know what to say, Diana pointed to her phone. "I take it you didn't see the news this morning."

I shook my head. "We had an incident at the retirement home. I was busy." The reminder had me silently hoping Nibs had behaved herself after I left.

Diana opened her phone and then swiped until she found what she was looking for.

It was a News Channel 2 breaking news story carrying a graphic image warning. The disturbing image was a distant shot of a small herd of wild horses lying dead amongst the sagebrush. The distance of the photo kept the gore from being seen clearly, but I could make out the white ribs of a couple of the horses glowing in the sun. The police were calling for any information on the incident. I turned aside, nauseated.

"No respect for nature. It's monstrous," Diana said, moving her phone away.

"Yes, it is," I barely got out, unsuccessfully trying to unsee the horror. Several years ago, a number of mustangs had been brutally shot and left for dead. But the picture in this article didn't look like the work of degenerate humans with guns. It looked more like the work of a large predator. But predators ate their prey. What animal slaughters a herd and leaves it to rot? Maybe monstrous was the right word.

The phone rang and Diana mouthed the words "see you tomorrow" before she gave a wave and moved off to answer it.

Too bad I couldn't let Diana in, because she'd probably make a really great friend.

I gave the room a once over to see if the thief had reappeared now that Diana was gone — he hadn't — then went to the glass case he'd been fiddling with. I crouched. The lock was sprung and the sliding door had been pulled open an inch. I'd need to tell someone to relock it, but I hesitated. When would I get the opportunity again to touch centuries old swords? Despite knowing all the protocols regarding how to handle artifacts, I pushed the sliding glass door wider and stuck my hand inside the case.

I wasn't supposed to touch artifacts.

And yet I couldn't stop. Every part of me hummed with an

energy that seemed to pull my hand closer until my fingertips reached the blade of the sword on the middle shelf.

Snap. The pop of static electricity exploded up my arm like I'd put my fingers on an electric fence. I pulled away but the tingling lingered. What was I thinking? I closed the glass door. Hopefully, no one saw my gigantic faux pas, or I could kiss my internship goodbye. Seeing that thief must have really addled my senses. I rubbed my hand on my slacks until the tingling stopped. Nothing good comes from dealing with the fae.

Chapter Three

It was only six o'clock when I left the museum, but the sun had dipped behind the mountains and cast the valley in a chilling shadow. The thief in black had not made another appearance. A very small part of me was disappointed; I would have liked to ask him if he really was over 1,000 years old. I didn't think he'd given up and I worried he'd try again, hiding better the next time.

I gave myself a mental shake. No, I needed to stop getting involved with Otherworld things. I'd already talked myself out of asking Nibs anything when I got home. Not my fae circus. Not my fae monkeys.

A zephyr wind raced between the buildings and slapped sharply against my back. I pulled on my down jacket I had carried to work for that very purpose. Everett had told me numerous times he could come to pick me up or I could drive the van if it was dark. But it's not that far to walk and I hate the idea of adding to his workload.

The large circular tower of the Brougher-Bath Victorian mansion rose like a specter against the dark sky. I smiled. Plus, if I drove I'd miss seeing the historic houses. Each one was like an old friend. I knew their lives almost as well as I knew my own.

A low rumble vibrated in the air.

I looked up. A storm rolling in? The darkening sky only held the crescent moon, no clouds. Of course, that didn't mean anything. Most days we have clear skies in Northern Nevada, but when we do get inclement weather, buckle up. I once saw it rain, then hail, then rain, then sleet, then snow, and then the sun came out and melted the snow before it snowed, again. Makes me seriously wonder if one of those hidden fae might just have power over the weather.

Another rumble filled the air, less like thunder and more like a growl, coming from behind me. Was there a mountain lion close? A bear? Wildlife didn't respect city boundaries here. Then I thought about the savaged mustangs and swallowed hard.

I looked over my shoulder into the falling night shadows. Movement between a garage and a house drew my gaze. Darkness seemed to slide over darkness. I heard the low rumble again. I squinted as if that would help me see the shape more clearly. This time the rumble rose to a snarl. Fear, like glue, held me rigid. I needed to stop thinking and start moving.

I forced one leg forward then the other.

Alternating between looking ahead and behind, I tried to walk as swiftly as possible without breaking into a run. I'd seen nature documentaries. Running equals chasing. But wait, wasn't I supposed to fall on the ground and hide my face if it was a bear? Or was it climb a tree?

I looked over my shoulder again. Out from between the buildings, I could finally make out a vague shape as it moved toward me, slowly but steadily. It resembled a large dog or wolf, but it moved like a bear, throwing its weight from side to side. The rumbling snarls paused every few moments and I could hear the creature pulling in air. Like it was sniffing. Like it was smelling its prey.

A car turned onto the road from a side street. Its headlights blinded me for a moment. Panic slammed my heart against my ribcage hard enough to steal my breath. I blinked furiously until I could see again. Shaking, I inhaled and picked up the pace.

The beast followed.

I reached for my cell to call animal control, but hesitated. There was no way the creature following me was a normal run-of-the-mill animal. It was fae. I knew it to my core. I thought about calling anyway. Animal control might scare it off. I'd look stupid, maybe even get in trouble for the prank call, but I wouldn't be dead.

But if this creature was the same one that killed the horses, I couldn't guarantee it wouldn't kill anyone that got in its way. What if I caused the death of civil servants just doing their job?

As much as something like this had always been a fear, I'd never been chased by a fae before. I was at a loss for what to do.

I noticed a group of teenagers farther down Curry Street, huddled close and laughing loudly, heading in my direction. They wouldn't see the fae beast through its glamour, but it would certainly notice them. Enough to give up its chase for a larger meal? I wasn't confident enough to chance it.

I let out a loud "Hey!" at the fae beast, then ran. The pounding of my feet echoed in the night air. Hopefully, loud enough to keep the fae beast's attention on me.

I turned down West Spear Street, straight past the Bougher-Bath mansion. Seconds spanned like hours as I alternated between looking ahead and looking behind, trying not to fall. Finally, the shadowed fae beast slinked around the corner, leaving the teenagers alone. I wasn't sure whether to be relieved or terrified I'd been successful.

It lifted its snout and drew in a large deep breath, smelling for me, then continued my way. It's lumbering shuffle picking up speed.

The adrenaline racing through my body amplified every sound.

The scratch of the fae beast's nails on the concrete seemed only inches away. Moments from tearing into my flesh.

A scream swelled, held inside only because I needed my breath for running.

Ahead, a dim porch light shone across the empty dirt front yard and through the bars of the Chartz House fence. A cast iron fence. According to Nibs, fae didn't like pure iron. Maybe if I could get over the fence, it might keep the fae beast at bay. Luckily, the house hadn't been occupied in a few years. No one would wonder what I was doing in their yard and call the police again. Long story.

Barely looking for cars, I dashed across the street toward potential safety.

The creature galloped now, snorting each time its massive paws slapped the ground.

Just as I reached the sidewalk on the other side the toe of my shoe caught the edge and I fell. My hands saved my face, but my right knee smashed into the concrete and the momentum drove me onto my side. I had no choice but to draw my legs in tight and throw my arms up to protect my head.

The snarling and scraping sounded almost on top of me. A slick rancid smell coated my throat, making me gag.

I was really going to die. More than die, I was going to be eaten.

I heard the creak of leather, the thunk of heavy tread, and the feel of fabric sliding across my back. I let out a squeak in surprise. I dared to lower my arms a few inches, and tried to scramble backwards as I looked up. I just made out the familiar dark form in a long coat and beanie in the moonlight and dim porch light.

Standing between me and the fae creature was the thief from the museum.

The creature slid to a stop only a couple feet away, silent. Massive, it definitely looked more like a wolf than a bear. With a grunt, it pulled itself up into a hunched position on its two back legs. I wished the beast would make up its mind on what it wanted to be, a wolf or a bear. Then, shockingly, it opened its snout and spoke with a heavy lisp. "Thep athide, I'm here for the girl."

Girl? As in me?

The thief shifted to block me from the fae beast even more. "What do you want with her?" he asked, clearly not shocked the creature could speak. Who was this guy? Trying not to use my shredded palms, I sat up and then stood. I sucked in a breath through clenched teeth as bursts of pain shot down my leg from my knee. I stopped myself from grabbing onto the thief for support. Just barely.

"Thep athide," the creature repeated. I peeked around the thief's shoulder.

"Is it a werewolf?" I asked out loud without thinking. The thief threw a scowl my way and pushed me back behind him.

"It's not a werewolf, it's an *ossorian*."

"What's that?"

"It is the thing currently trying to harm you. Stay behind me," he snapped.

"I don't even know you." And what were the odds he would show up right when I was heading home? Creepy and a thief. "Wait, were you following me?"

He looked at me with an irritated expression and opened his mouth possibly to speak just as the *ossorian* barreled straight into him. There was no time to evade or even brace against the attack. We all hurled backwards. The thief and *ossorian* slammed into me and then we all slammed into the iron fence. My shoulder, back, and head hit in quick succession.

Crushed against the fence under the combined weight of the thief and the *ossorian*, I couldn't take a breath. Spots exploded behind my eyes. Through the ringing in my ears, I heard the thief give a massive groan, and the next moment the heavy weight of both he and the *ossorian* disappeared. I slid to the ground, gulping in a lung full of air and coughing it back out again. The next breath was easier.

I grabbed the fence and pulled myself up, touching the back of my head. I hissed when I found a tender spot.

The thief stood near. I watched him reach over his shoulder as if to grab a weapon, and only grasp air. At that moment, the *ossorian* lunged again. The thief stuck out his gloved hands, catching both sides of its mouth. He held the monster at arm's length as the *ossorian* flailed its hairy arms. Its hands — paws — whichever, with thick dark fingers ending in talons, rent the air trying to find purchase. Spittle flew from his snapping jaws and some landed on my arm. I was never wearing that coat again.

"Are you well?" the thief called over his shoulder.

What? Was I well? He's the one holding back a slavering beast! I nodded, which he couldn't see.

"I say, are you well?" he called again.

"Yes" I croaked.

The thief and *ossorian* shuffled closer. I stepped back and found myself up against the fence again, the cold of the metal quickly seeping through the fabric to chill my skin. The beast snarled loud enough to make my chest vibrate and the thief lost his grip on the *ossorian's* face. Its maw fell to the thief's shoulder. The sound of the beast ravaging flesh and the thief's cry was going to haunt me forever.

They fell toward me and I dived out of the way.

The thief hit the fence first but used the *ossorian's* momentum to roll until the fae beast was the one up against the iron. Steam rose into the air. The sound of sizzling meat echoed loudly in the night. The *ossorian* let go of the thief's shoulder and released an almost human scream before it crumpled to the ground.

Nibs was right. Fae and iron didn't mix.

The thief stumbled and cradled his injured arm. He looked over at me, his eyes bright with pain. "You need to run."

No doubt he was right. I mean, there was a fae beast — *ossorian*, whatever — on the ground and I was pretty sure it would rip me to pieces if it got the chance but running seemed wrong.

The thief was — well, a thief — but that didn't mean he should die. Especially not while trying to keep me safe. I looked around hoping to find a fallen tree branch or a large rock, some kind of weapon so I could help, instead of just being a damsel in distress.

The guy grabbed one of the metal fence posts with his gloved hand and yanked it away from the rest of the fence and out of the ground like a popsicle stick.

Holy crap.

Maybe he didn't need my help after all.

The thief aimed the decorative pointed end of the fence post toward the *ossorian* like a spear. The *ossorian,* still lying on the ground, rolled closer to the thief's legs. Reaching out with a snarl, it pulled the thief down on top of it, who cried out as teeth again found his mangled shoulder. The iron fence post clattered to the sidewalk.

I rushed to grab it. Raising it like a baseball bat, I swung and slammed it across the beast's back. The iron seemed to sink into the skin. I gagged. The *ossorian* howled, yet continued to attack the thief. I yanked the rod from its skin with a sucking pop — definitely going to vomit-- to hit it again. The beast whirled away from the thief to face me, its new target, blood dripping from its jowls.

Its large taloned hand pulled the fence post from my grip.

I stumbled backward.

Suddenly, the thief appeared on the *ossorian's* back and his arms wrapped around its neck. The *ossorian* tried to dislodge the thief from his chokehold. They fell against the fence again and both ended up on the ground where they grappled. The beast and the man wrestled. Between one moment and the next, the thief wrested the iron rod from the claws of the fae beast and then thrust it into its body. The *ossorian* fell to the ground twitching.

The thief stood, his movements unsteady and his chest heaving. He looked down at the *ossorian.* I stared, too. The air shimmered around the fallen fae beast. The shimmer grew stronger until the body melted and reshaped. Soon it was no longer the form of the fae beast, but a naked man. A dead, pale-skinned man with dark hair and a fence post embedded deep in his chest.

"You killed him," I whispered through dry lips. There was an actual dead guy on the ground. My stomach twisted and sweat burst over my chest and back, chilling me.

"Yes," the thief answered, his tone weak.

I definitely did not make enough money for the amount of therapy I would need.

I dragged my gaze away from the dead body to glance at the thief. He swayed as he stared down. With a jerking movement, he raised his right hand in a fist and knocked it against his chest right below his mangled shoulder. He winced in pain. "May you follow Donn's horn to Teach Duinn and find peace," he said, his voice husky and weak.

Then faceplanted on the ground at my feet.

I looked down at the thief and then over at the other body.

"Ummmm... "

Chapter Four

Grandpa wasn't a cold man. He had given hugs before bed. He laughed. He smiled. I was never in doubt he genuinely loved me and my grandma. In my mind, I wondered if he might have been better than having a dad, because Grandpa made rules, but let me break them all the time.

Except one rule. That rule was solid and unyielding, and I learned it on my first day of kindergarten.

During recess, I had noticed what Nibs later said was probably a pixie flying around the sandbox. I sat down with the other five-year-olds who were creating castles and moats and told them we should build a special house for the "fairy." We played happily until one of the kids demanded I prove there was a fairy. Eventually, it escalated into hair-pulling and kicking.

When Grandpa came to pick me up from the office, I was afraid he'd be angry, but he looked down at me with so much sadness, I begged him to tell me how to make it better. He was silent all the way to the car. After buckling me into my car seat, he climbed in the driver's side and stared out of the windshield.

Finally, he turned his head to me. "You don't see things that aren't there, okay?" His voice was firm.

"Why couldn't the other kids see the fairy?" I asked.

"Because it isn't there. Because it can't be there. It's *dangerous* for it to be there. Do you understand?"

For a moment, I sat there not understanding at all. I'd clearly seen a fairy. It had been just as real as the other kids playing in the sand next to me. Grandpa's eyes bore into me and suddenly it made sense. Not completely, but at five I understood enough. I knew that day Grandpa saw things too. We were the same. And because of that, Grandpa was afraid. I looked at him in the rearview mirror. "I don't see things that aren't there, Grandpa."

He nodded, satisfied, turned the car on and drove us home. I decided not to mention what I'd overheard the office ladies say. But I did wonder if seeing things no one else could was my punishment for not having parents. Later, I learned it was punishment for being born a Wylde.

That night at dinner we ate dessert first and I stayed up later than my bedtime to play another round of our card game. Rules were still bent and broken all the time, but Grandpa never had to pick me up from school again for seeing something "that wasn't there."

Except I wasn't sure how even Grandpa would have been able to pretend there wasn't a dead guy with a fence post in his chest and another guy, probably dead too, at my feet.

My stomach tried to roll upward, but I swallowed hard.

Should I run home and lock the door behind me? That seemed like the smart decision. I needed to stay out of Otherworld business. Dead bodies or not, this had nothing to do with me. I brushed aside the memory of the *ossorian* lisping his intention to take me. That had to have been a mistake.

One of the bodies moved and I stifled a scream. I jumped back, my sore knee nearly buckling, as the thief tried to roll onto his side. He didn't make it and fell back onto his face with a moan.

Walk away, Genny. The thief being alive changed nothing. The fae world was dangerous. Hadn't Grandpa spent my whole life telling me so? Hadn't I just been nearly eaten by a fae beast? The thief groaned again. It seemed ungrateful to just leave him on the ground, even if he did just kill someone. He had protected me, after all. And followed me like a creep. And tried to steal a sword from my museum.

I sighed.

I turned my body so the dead guy was not in my line of vision and knelt. "I'm going to try and get you turned over, okay?" He mumbled something in reply. I decided to take it as an affirmative. I gripped the stiff fabric of his long coat and heaved. He growled with pain as his injured shoulder rolled under him and he fell face up on the ground.

"Gods," he hissed. His eyes pinched closed with pain.

I winced. "Sorry."

On his back, his injuries could be seen more clearly. Beneath the open coat, torn fabric lay in shreds over his shoulder. Blood, black in the darkness, oozed and already covered much of his side.

He opened his eyes and locked on mine. His pupils were so large in the low light only the barest ring of his gold irises could be seen. His black beanie had been lost. His shaggy blonde hair curled wildly and with abandon. Long tracts of glinting sweat dripped from his forehead and rolled over his high cheekbones. His lips parted as he let out a shaky breath. This time the twist in my stomach was not from fear. Seriously, did I have any good sense left? Thief-murderer-stalkers should not be found attractive.

The thief tried to sit up and failed. He touched his injured shoulder and grimaced. "We must away."

"Were you following me?" I asked, staring down at him.

He blinked. "You wish to talk of this now?"

"It's a simple answer. Yes, or no?"

"It is not a simple answer." He paused and looked guilty. "But yes. Not at first, but I became bothered by unanswered questions. I found you just as the *ossorian* gave chase. I will answer anything you wish, but we must not stay any longer."

"What about him?" I jabbed my thumb over my shoulder in the direction of the dead guy. I didn't look, but I still felt the urge to vomit.

Headlights from a passing car illuminated the corner. I froze. How could I even explain what had happened? This curse was going to cause me more trouble than it already had one day. But the *ossorian* must have retained its glamour even after death because the car didn't stop or even slow down.

"That is why we cannot stay. The others will come to fetch their fallen brother."

The thief didn't look like he was up for another round. He'd barely survived this first one. Without him, I certainly wouldn't survive another either. My knee throbbed in agreement.

I opened my mouth knowing Grandpa would say I was a "glutton for punishment," and also that I was being stupid. Both would be a fair assessment. "I live near here and there are medical supplies."

"I would be in your debt," he said as he attempted to sit up again. I reached out to help and he pulled back like my hand was poison. "It's fine. I will manage."

I lowered my hand and stood. "Toxic masculinity is harmful. Guys can ask for help."

"An enlightened time, no doubt." He gained his feet but swayed dangerously. "Aengus," he said as he dipped his head.

"What?"

"In my time, a person should introduce themselves. My name is Aengus."

Aengus sounded like a Scottish name. Was that the accent I heard? "Umm right, well I'm Imogen Wylde, Genny."

He tried to bow, but nearly fell forward. Frustration tightened his expression, but his words were soft. "It is a pleasure to meet you, Imogen."

I couldn't help smiling in response. I'd met guys who'd tried to sound gallant and knightly, and it had fallen flat. From Aengus it felt natural. Like he'd behaved that way all his life. He'd implied he was over 1,000 years old. Maybe he had. I wanted to ask if it was the truth but stayed silent. My gaze dropped unbidden to the dead body on the ground and I shuddered. What was I getting myself into?

We made our slow way toward the retirement home. I watched Aengus intently, convinced every wobble or stumble he would fall. There was no way I would be able to carry him by myself, even if I wasn't limping. Scrutinizing Aengus meant I wasn't watching my own way in places where the sidewalk was uneven. I tripped and bounced off of more than one tree trunk.

Aengus glanced at me. "I will not fall," he assured, "but if you hurt yourself, I am in no condition to help."

My face flushed with embarrassment. Luckily, it was too dark for him to see my red cheeks. I forced myself to stop staring at him and focused on getting home in one piece.

Just as we reached the house, the howl of wolves carried in the air. The dead guy's brethren? I wondered if glamour would suppress the sound. Or if the locals would hear and gossip about it tomorrow.

The porch lights were on and the night nurse read a book at the front desk. Everything seemed quiet. Whatever Nibs had done to make the residents disruptive must have worn off quicker than she'd predicted. We made our way through the side gate to the back of the house. With every step, Aengus seemed to place each foot slower and more ponderously. I was worried he would pass out, but he continued to move. We reached the ramp. Aengus grabbed the railing with his good arm and leaned hard as he made his way forward.

Finally, we reached the top. I stepped up to the door and opened it inward. "Come inside and I'll get some bandages." Aengus shuffled past me, past the island and made his way to the small kitchen table. With little grace, he fell into one of the chairs barely catching himself before he could topple over the other side.

Mostly certain of his stability in the chair, I left the kitchen to grab medical supplies. Our infirmary consisted of one bed, a hanging curtain and a wall of cupboards, many with locks for controlled substances. Only the chandelier above remained of what had once been the formal dining room.

Not sure what Aengus would need, I grabbed some of whatever we had in the bandage drawer and swiped a whole bottle of rubbing alcohol. I'd need to remember to put it on the reorder list. I really needed that assistant. Hopefully, the residents and attendants stayed where they were for a while yet. I didn't want to try and explain the bleeding guy in the kitchen. It helped that most of the residents went to bed at four in the afternoon.

When I returned, Aengus was trying and failing to remove his long trench coat.

I dropped the supplies on the table and moved to help. "No!" Aengus snapped just as I laid a hand on the fabric. I stumbled back as I let go, grabbing the table. What the hell?

He raised his gloved hand out in front of him and took a deep breath. "My apologies. You must not touch my skin."

Definitely not the explanation I was expecting.

"Why?" I asked. It was probably a very rude question, but I couldn't help asking. Suddenly the whole head to toe wardrobe made a little more sense. Was he a germaphobe? Did he hate being touched?

"Because in my current state, you would die," he said in all seriousness.

I blinked in disbelief. There was no reason to be melodramatic, but I didn't argue. I stood back as he managed to get out of the coat, dropping it to the floor. The shirt beneath was torn to shreds on one side. Only a thin strip kept it from completely falling off. He pulled the tattered fabric over his head and dropped it next to the coat.

On one side, he looked like a well-muscled athlete, lean and strong.

On the other side, the entire top of his shoulder looked as if someone had taken a hatchet to it, leaving deep ragged grooves that continued to ooze blood. There were also deep slashes on his side. I did not notice washboard abs, because that would be wrong. Dirt and blood ran down his arm and chest and I could see now his pants were shiny with blood. Low riding pants.

Aengus reached for the rolled gauze.

"Wait," I said not able to watch him do such a poor job at first aid. Animal scratches were nasty. "You need to at least disinfect it." I pointed to the rubbing alcohol.

"It's fine," he assured me. "I only need to stop the bleeding." He bent his head and held the end of the gauze against his shoulder with his chin. He used the whole roll, but when he got to the end he seemed unsure how to hold it closed.

"Here." I grabbed the surgical tape and moved toward him.

Aengus leaned away.

"I won't touch your skin. I'll just put a few strips of tape so the gauze doesn't move." He contemplated for a moment, then gave a small nod. I unrolled a strip and bit it off. Carefully, I applied it to the gauze, then added two more.

"I need to rest, to heal," Aengus said weakly. I watched his eyelids sink and jerk upwards a couple times as he spoke. Getting attacked by a large fae beast and having his shoulder and side torn up seemed like too elaborate a scheme just to get into my bed, but I hesitated. Aengus appeared to sway. If he passed out at the table there was no way I could carry him, even if he let me touch him, and I wouldn't be able to explain what he was doing there if I left him at the table.

"My room is right over there." I pointed. Aengus barely got to his feet and stumbled toward it. I grabbed up the trench coat and bloody shirt from the floor and ran ahead to open the door. I stepped aside as he slowly made his way to my bed. Without a word he fell on it, face first, unmoving.

For the first time in my life there was a man in my bed. Too bad he was a thief, murderer, and currently dripping blood all over my duvet.

Chapter Five

"He's rather ugly," Nibs mumbled as she glared down at Aengus from the pillow near the head of the bed. The cowboy hat was gone and instead of the pink ballgown she wore doll-sized overalls and a multicolored scrap of cloth wound around her neck like a scarf.

"Do you think so?" I asked, only giving Nibs a quick glance over my shoulder before I turned back to my desk and continued to read on my laptop. Which I'd been doing for most of the night. My head and knee had taken turns aching even after pain killers and sleeping on the floor held no appeal. Plus, every time I closed my eyes, I could see the fae beast snarling. Followed by its dead body. Then a cold sweat would break out and I'd fight away nausea. Sleep had been impossible.

"Oh yes." Nibs continued her tone pitying. "He has hair on his head. And his skin! No spots or bumps at all. And those bulgy shoulders, so ugly."

I swiveled my desk chair around and raised my eyebrows. "You're mostly just describing a human. A human like me."

The Brownie leaned back against the headboard and shook her head slowly. "I know, so sad."

With an eye roll, I turned back around and continued to read.

I had tried to get ahead on retirement home business but was immediately foiled by the banking software — again. Pivoting, I started looking for information on the origins of the swords in the case I'd caught Aengus tampering with. I'm pretty good at web searching, I've looked for evidence regarding my mom for years. I'm almost positive my lack of information had more to do with her ability to hide and less about my skills. For other members of my extended family, I had files full. The one about my Great-Great Aunt Imogen was especially full.

Truthfully, I'd first tried to look up *ossorians*, but when I couldn't figure out the spelling I put in "wolf beasts." That only brought up fictional examples and some very eye-opening kink videos. The name Aengus didn't bring up anything useful either. So, I focused on the swords, specifically the sword that Aengus seemed to be the most interested.

I found an article on an UK news website from a little over a year ago. A tomb had been uncovered near the city of Sterling by a farmer who had sold the ancient sword to a collector in the States before studies could be made. The farmer did, however, open the empty tomb to archeologists. There was a bit of a kerfluffle over the missing human remains but the farmer insisted that the body was there when he took the sword. With no money trail as there had been with the farmer's sale of the sword, the archeologists were forced to blame grave robbers. Even without the body, they'd been able to date the tomb from around 450 to 500 c.e.

What did all that have to do with the guy on my bed?

I turned in my chair again and stared at Aengus. My gaze found his low-riding tactical pants and I forced myself to look further up, but the lean muscles over his back were just as distracting, so I focused on his wounded shoulder.

Overnight, blood had leaked through the gauze, but from the dark brown color, it seemed to have stopped. I was relieved that not taking him to a hospital had been the right call. I hadn't been sure as he hadn't moved at all overnight. But Nibs said the hospital couldn't help fae. He still didn't look fae to me. He just looked human. A human whose skin appeared leached of color and whose slightly parted lips looked purplish. His breathing had stayed consistent, but each breath in and out seemed slow.

A knock reverberated through my door. I jolted, my whole body clenched, and I stifled a yelp. If someone came in, they couldn't miss Aengus's bloody body sleeping on my bed. I jumped up from the chair and rushed to the door to lean against it. "Not dressed!" I called.

"No worries. Just wanted to remind you Mr. Friedman's dental appointment is at nine this morning," Everett said from the other side. In all the crazy, I'd forgotten about my actual responsibilities. Filled with guilt, I checked my phone. It was quarter after eight. At least I'd showered and dressed in the bathroom down the hall before the sun had risen. The cold sweat had made me feel gross. With a house full of people and only two full bathrooms, I've learned to take showers before the residents wake up.

"I'll be out in ten," I assured him and listened for him to walk away before I moved.

I looked toward the bed. The knocking and loud voices hadn't stirred Aengus. If I couldn't occasionally see his back rise as he breathed, I might have worried he was dead. I still worried he'd lost too much blood.

I grabbed one of my shoes off the floor and tapped Aengus on the leg with it. When he didn't move, I tapped harder. Nothing. I stopped and slipped the shoe on my foot. Then worked the other one on while grabbing up my purse. "Nibs, I have to go. Can you make sure he doesn't go wandering out of the room if he wakes up while I'm gone?" The Brownie reached out her hand, palm up. "I don't have any sugar now, but I'll make sure to bring you a big bag of gummy bears when I come back." Appeased, she sat cross-legged on the pillow. Her dark eyes stared unblinking at Aengus.

I walked out, leaving Nibs in charge. Which was honestly probably the weirdest thing to happen in the last two days.

"Oh wow, it's been ages! How are you?" the hygienist directed at me with a very large, white smile when she came out into the waiting room to lead Mr. Friedman back for his appointment. She was new. Her name tag said Shelby. I remembered a girl from high school that vaguely resembled the woman in front of me.

"I'm good," I answered without prompting more from her. My nickname had been Genny Weird back then. I had no desire to catch up, or worse, reminisce. I could already feel my anxiety skyrocketing. I tried to ground myself. The tile floor beneath my feet. The stiff back of the waiting room chair. The hum of the heating system above me.

Shelby was not swayed. "My husband and I just moved back here. I wondered if I'd run into anyone I used to know. I never expected it to be Genny Wylde." My face must have clearly asked the question "why" because she immediately explained. "I thought for sure you'd be doing one of those shows. You know where the person points to the audience and tells them what their dead loved ones are saying."

"A television psychic?" I barely got out.

"Yes! Exactly! Remember that day you said hello to Mrs. Randall's husband and she nearly passed out because he'd died the week before? Didn't she give you like a month of detention for that? I mean I don't know if you can actually *see dead people*," Shelby curved her fingers into quotes, "but I thought you were believable. Do you do like ghost tours now or anything?"

I just blinked, unable to respond.

Shelby smiled large again. "Well anyways it was really great to see you again." She turned to Mr. Friedman. "Shall we get this show on the road?"

Mr. Friedman, his circle of white hair sticking out in all directions around the bald spot on his head and his glasses threatening to fall off his nose, adjusted his walker and followed her into the back.

I'd never had anyone react to me the way that Shelby just had. I wasn't sure if it was a good thing or a bad one. It was certainly interesting but my plate was too full at the moment to focus on trying to understand it. I sat down in a chair and pulled out my phone.

With nothing to do for the next half hour, I researched more on the tomb and sword. Many articles were behind a paywall, so I scrolled around what was readily available. One clickbait story caught my eye —*Tomb of Round Table Knight Found!*. Valid or not, it was going to be a while, so good old curiosity had me clicking on it.

The story repeated much of the basic information I already knew, but this article mentioned an Arthurian scholar who had translated some possible Ogham script carved into the side of the tomb's stone wall. Roughly it said, "Sealed within, the sword Caliburn and the Fallen Guardian, Beloved of the Dux."

I googled Caliburn. The very first site to pop up proclaimed Caliburn to be Excalibur and every additional article said about the same thing. Disney and a few fantasy novels in my teenage years provided the extent of my King Arthur knowledge. I knew the main players and a few common plot points. What I didn't know was how it all connected to the fae.

I couldn't trust the click-bait article, I knew that, but my mind ran in circles with what I'd found.

Was the sword Excalibur resting in a glass case in our museum?

That couldn't be possible, right? I mean, first Excalibur was a fictional creation. And what about the man in my bed? He said the sword was his. Did that mean he was King Arthur? But he said his name was Aengus. And if the inscription on the tomb was accurate, where was the buried Guardian? And what did any of this have to do with almost being eaten last night?

For the remainder of the wait, I oscillated between excitement and disbelief until I remembered none of it mattered. I needed to keep out of fae business. The Otherworld only meant trouble. Aengus would rest up and then leave, taking all the crazy shit with him.

Then my life would go back to normal.

Of course, normal meant being a friendless orphan who still saw ghosts and fae, but at least I could ignore them in peace.

Mr. Friedman hobbled back out with his walker into the waiting room with Shelby. "Don't forget to take my card and call sometime. We should do brunch," she offered seemingly unironically before she grabbed the next patient waiting.

Mr. Friedman scheduled his next cleaning and then I helped him out the door and back into the van. I secured the walker in the back and hopped into the driver's seat. "You should call her. You don't have any friends," Mr. Friedman said bluntly.

I laughed at the idea. "What are you talking about? I have a whole house full of friends."

The harumph from Mr. Friedman clearly conveyed his disagreement but also his pleasure about being called a friend.

All the residents were really wonderful people and I loved them, but in the end, I couldn't truly be honest with them. Really, I wasn't just cursed to see things the rest of the population couldn't, I was also isolated because of it, too.

A late morning quiet lay over the historical district as we headed north up Division Street. Commuters had already left and lunchtime traffic hadn't started. The only car I saw as we headed back home was two streets down, heading toward the main street. It was so quiet in fact, a doe stepped out in the road, her fawn skittering beside her, and demanded we wait while she tip-toed across. The idyllic picture made it hard to believe the horror that had happened last night.

My whole body went cold at the memory.

My greatest fear had literally unfolded like a nightmare. Seeing the fae was bad enough, but having them notice me back and want to harm me? Utterly terrifying! I really hoped Aengus had halted whatever scheme that had made the fae attack me by killing the *ossorian*. How horrible did it make me to be happy someone was dead?

Just as we passed Third Street, Mr. Friedman's glasses finally toppled to the floor. He bent over to retrieve them and cried out as he sat back up, pointing at the side mirror. I jerked the wheel in surprise and hastily corrected. I shot a quick glance at the mirror and then over my shoulder.

An *ossorian* galloped behind us, gaining with every stride. How had Mr. Friedman...

"Let's shake a leg!" he cried beside me and I realized I'd taken my foot off the gas.

I pushed my confusion away and slammed my foot down on the pedal.

Out from between two street-parked cars, a second *ossorian* leaped in front of the van.

I braked hard. The van fishtailed. Tires squealed. The whole vehicle rocked to a stop as the hood came within inches of the fae beast.

The greasy-haired *ossorian* raised up onto his back legs. Hunched and upright, I could clearly see its bloodshot eyes and snarling mouth. I thought of the dead guy last night, the fence post driven into his chest. Aengus had said others would come for the corpse. Were these them and were they still after me? Was there a man beneath this beast as well? Or a woman?

Something hit the back windshield. Both Mr. Friedman and I screamed. I threw a glance over my shoulder and saw the other *ossorian* had caught up with us. Talons rent the metal with a horrible squeal. A snarl ripped from the beast loud enough to be heard through the glass as it clung to the frame. The *ossorian* in front slammed its hands down onto the hood. The screech of its talons added to the cacophony. Mr. Friedman looked over at me, his eyes wide and terrified. "Go!" he bellowed.

I hit the gas.

The *ossorian* in front slid down the grill. Half its body bounced against the road between the front wheels, its talons still locked into the hood. "Swerve!" Mr. Friedman continued to direct. I followed his lead. I turned the wheel and the beast's body was pulled under one of the front wheels. His talons ripped free. The van bounced over his body and the whole vehicle threatened to tip on its side. A moment later, we popped over it with the back wheels. Still upright, we continued speeding down the street.

Another vehicle drove down the street, headed in the opposite direction. The ossorian holding onto the rear of the van was still there. The car sped on by without pause.

Alone on the street, I braked again and heard it scrambling, trying to hold on. I sent us forward once more, swerving from one side of the road to the other. The beast finally lost purchase and slid off. I watched in the rearview as it slammed down onto the asphalt and rolled.

I didn't slow down.

"I hate those fae bastards," Mr. Friedman grumbled beside me. *What?!*

It had occurred to me that Mr. Friedman had seen something he shouldn't be able to, but knowing they were fae. How?

I sat there, silent. He pushed his glasses back up against his face and looked out all the mirrors, then turned his whole body to glance out the back window. He nodded to himself as he plopped back down forward in his seat. "They're gone." He gestured toward the street. "Let's get home. The wards will protect us." He didn't even look my way. He was acting as if he hadn't just completely destroyed my reality.

I'd drive us home, but when we got there no way was he getting out of some serious explaining.

He sighed and reached over to pat my hand affectionately. It felt apologetic. "It was a stipulation of living in this house. I promised your grandparents I'd keep the secret. I've already said too much."

"My grandparents are dead. Whatever promise you made to them is dead, too. Please tell me what's going on." I knew there was desperation in my voice, but beneath that layer anger simmered. My life suddenly felt like a mine field, another bomb going off with every new bit of information learned. How many people had lied to me?

Mr. Friedman shook his head against my reasoning. "You must speak with Jane. She leads the coven. We'll follow what she decides."

"Coven? As in witches?" The squeak of my voice hurt my own ears. Any more new information and my unraveling life was going to be just a pile of rubble.

"I can't say more. You must speak with Jane."

I heard the finality in his tone and I wanted to scream. Why was my life always questions and never answers? "But her dementia?"

"There are good days," he assured me. "Ask her then."

Defeated, I held the door as Mr. Friedman shuffled over the threshold and made his slow way toward the front room where the TV blared Jeopardy reruns. Everett appeared out of the hallway and bypassed the walker. He gave Mr. Friedman a nod as he passed.

"Everything go well?" he asked.

I froze and my eyes glanced through the kitchen window to the parked van. I could clearly see the rents in the hood, but from this angle, I could also see the deep scratches all over the back of the van. Everett followed my gaze. "What the hell?" he said barely above a whisper.

I said the first thing that came to mind. "Bear." Bears were common. Especially when they're bulking up for hibernation. Although, I've never heard of one attacking a car before.

He turned back toward me. "Bear?"

"Eeeeyup," I answered, putting a loud pop on the end of the word. I even rocked back and forth from heel to toe. Nothing to hide here, nope nothing at all. Everett opened his mouth to probably question me further.

Suddenly, Mr. Friedman's voice called from the middle of the hall. "Biggest damn bear I ever saw. Our Genny has nerves of steel. Lucky to be alive."

Everett's eyes widened. I could feel my face flush with embarrassment and panic. "Glad you guys are safe. Does our insurance even cover bear attack?"

I shrugged with a wince. "Maybe? I'll call and find out."

He patted my shoulder then headed back toward the front room, talking under his breath. "Bears attacking vans? That's some real crazy shit."

I moved so I could see down the hallway. Mr. Friedman slowly made his way. He turned and gave me a small salute.

If I listened hard enough, I imagined my whole world exploding around me. A hysterical laugh almost escaped as I turned the doorknob to my room. I slipped quickly inside and leaned against the back of door, breathing like I really had been run down by a bear or more accurately, an *ossorian*... again.

Aengus still lay on the bed, chest down. It looked like Nibs had stayed exactly where I'd left her, too. Oh no, I forgot the gummy bears! Failing to provide promised items to a Brownie is a recipe for misery. Ask me how I know. She immediately noticed the lack of sugary snacks. She scowled and leaped to her feet.

I put up my hands in surrender. "Double the next time I go out, I promise."

She narrowed her eyes.

"Triple."

She acceded with a nod and sat back down.

I walked closer to the bed. Aengus was young. I hadn't noticed that last night with all the snarling and the fighting and the bleeding. Despite the sallowness greying his skin, Aengus's face appeared unlined and smooth. If he was over thirty, I'd be shocked. But he could be. He might even be over a thousand. Did all fae stay so young in appearance? I caught myself before I reached out and ran a hand along the ridge of his sharp cheekbone. "Has he moved at all?"

"First his eyes lids moved, pinky moved on his left hand, then his right hand curled and uncurled, mouth opened then closed..."

I sighed. Nibs could be very literal. "I meant, like sat up or went to the bathroom or said something."

"No."

"Okay." I stepped to my desk. I pulled out my phone from my back pocket and set it down. Then I swiveled the chair to be able to sit and keep watch. Remembering more of my adult responsibilities, I reached behind and grabbed my phone.

> Having a rough time — if it's all right I'm going to do as you suggested and take some time off

Diana texted back almost immediately.

> Of course! I wished you'd taken it sooner, but I really hope it helps

I felt a little guilty, even if it wasn't technically a lie. Last night and today had certainly been rough. To relieve some guilt, I sent one more text.

> Drinks at the Old Globe on me when I get back

Then I logged into the van's insurance policy, hoping there was a destruction by wildlife deductible, but couldn't focus. The silence drove me stir crazy. Finally, unable to just sit and stare at the guy in my bed, I looked at Nibs and asked the question. "Why didn't you tell me the residents could see you?"

Nibs looked down and fiddled with her scarf and adjusted the buckles on her overalls. "Only when I let them," she mumbled.

"They only can see you if you let them?"

She nodded. "Or if... " she trailed off.

"Nibs?"

"Or if they have a Sul Aos Si."

It sounded like she said a sool ees shee. "What is that?"

"It's a talisman that allows a human to see through glamour." Aengus said half muffled against the comforter. "It's what I thought you had."

I stood up at the sound of his voice and took a step toward him. "How do you feel?" He raised his gloved hand to stop me from coming closer.

"I am well," he said as he started to lever himself up, his arm muscles and back straining. Aengus had looked young as he slept, but his movements now were as halted and careful as the elderly residents living in the house. I had a feeling he was as far from *well* as it got. Once he managed to sit, he held his injured arm against his bare chest and ran his other hand over his golden hair. The muscles along his arm and shoulder rounded and swelled.

It was like he was doing the whole sexy injured hero thing on purpose. Or was he the villain? He had tried to commit a felony. Villains should not save people from wolf beasts, get injured, and end up half naked in people's beds. It made things very confusing. Was the room warm? It really felt warm. I needed to open the window. My gaze shifted back to the bed and Aengus was staring at me... and get the man a shirt!

I cracked the window and a brisk fall wind rushed through and tousled Aengus's hair. This was getting ridiculous. My gaze dropped to the bandages around his shoulder and side.

"I'll be right back. I'm going to get some more bandages so we can change yours." I took a step toward the door. Nibs scrambled down the comforter to follow.

Aengus probed his shoulder, then said, "That is not necessary." He tried to stand but only got a few inches up before he settled back down onto the mattress.

"You have to change them or the wound will get infected."

With a wan smile, he shook his head. "Trust me. The wound is healing fine."

It wasn't like I could sit on him and force him to change the bandages. A picture flashed in my mind of me straddling him as I forced a bandage change. I abruptly dropped onto the computer chair and deliberately thought about last night instead. Nibs crawled into my lap. "Maybe you can answer the questions you didn't last night because you passed out."

"Only if I may ask my own," he said.

"Fine. Why were you following me?" I wanted to ask him about the *ossorians* and the sword that might be Excalibur, but I needed that question answered first.

"I wanted to know how you saw through my glamour. As I said when I awoke, I thought you had a Sul Aos Si, but you clearly saw the *ossorian* and you did not have it on you last night. It can only mean you have fae blood in your lineage."

All the air left my chest in a huff of surprise. "That's not possible," I whispered.

"And yet it is the only explanation."

I'd spent my whole life trying to keep out the fae. They and their world were dangerous, Grandpa made sure I understood that. And I certainly learned it last night and this morning. Would he really have railed against the fae if we were... related? It couldn't possibly be true. I looked down at Nibs. She wouldn't look me in the eye.

"Do you know who your fae ancestor might be?" Aengus asked

gently. "Many families have a story or legend passed down that speaks of it."

"No, nothing like that." All the family history I'd uncovered had only proved that the Wyldes had never quite fit in but hadn't been clear on the why. But Grandpa definitely had the ability to see through glamour. The family trait had to come from somewhere. Uncertainty traveled like bugs under my skin. I fought the urge to stand and pace to release the tension. I needed to think about something else.

I looked back at Aengus and asked the first question that came to mind. "Are you fae?"

He shook his head. "I am like you. Or I was. On my mother's side. Her mother, my grandmother, had a fae lover. I did not know my lineage until the *custos* took me in. But I am *custos* no longer." His words were wooden, but I could hear the sadness swirling beneath them. Without thinking I reached out to comfort.

"Do you not listen!" Aengus snapped pulling away.

My face heated to a dark shade of crimson. Mission accomplished. I no longer worried about my lineage. I now worried I'd melt into a pile of embarrassment. "Why can't I touch you?" As the words left me, I wanted to take them back. "I'm sorry, forget I asked. It was rude."

Aengus looked away and reached for the trench coat lying on the end of the bed. He carefully pulled it on over his injured arm, sans shirt, and sighed, his tone softer. "It was not rude. I just do not wish to speak about it." Awkwardly, he maneuvered his other arm into its sleeve. When the coat was completely on he tried to stand and sank back down. He pointed at Nibs. "You should ask who sent your Brownie. That might answer where your fae blood comes from."

"What do you mean ask Nibs who sent her?" I alternated between looking at Nibs in my lap and Aengus on the bed.

"Brownies are not free agents. They either go where their master sends them or where their queen does."

Master? Queen? I looked at Nibs. "Did someone send you?" She winced, but nodded. "Who sent you Nibs?" She didn't answer. "Who?" I demanded.

She cringed. "Your father."

Chapter Seven

I only have one memory of my mother that isn't fabricated from pictures or stories my grandparents told me. Which is odd since I know she was with me until I was five. I'm in a car. It's long like a station wagon and I'm buckled into a car seat behind the passenger side. My mom is driving. We've driven for, what feels to me, like hours. There were buildings and other cars before, but now there is just a rocky desert and mountains. I don't think we're on a road, it's just dirt out the windshield, and the whole car shakes and bounces. At one point, my teeth clack together on my tongue and I cry. My mom reaches a hand back and I grab ahold of it. I don't let go and she keeps driving, one hand on the wheel. Occasionally, she looks back across the bridge of our arms to smile at me. There are tears in her eyes.

That's all I have, one memory, but at least I've got it. My father was a tabula rasa, I didn't even have a name. By the time I started kindergarten, I was without a father and a mother. Grandma and Grandpa were my only family.

And now there was just me.

"What do you mean, my father sent you?" Disbelief weakened

my words. If my father had *sent* Nibs, that meant he knew I existed. A sinking feeling threatened to pull me down to the floor. I knew my mom had chosen to leave me, but I'd always secretly believed my father never knew he had a daughter. When I was younger, I fantasized he'd find out and come find me.

"Who is my father?" Anger and confusion hardened my tone.

"She may have been compelled not to say."

I looked toward Aengus sitting on the bed. He held out his hand like he was offering a snack, his tone conversational.

"Merely a theory, but if he sent a Brownie instead of coming himself there is certainly a reason. Likely of the dangerous variety."

Nibs slid down my legs to the floor and scurried to the cracked open window. "We're not done, Nibs." I stood up, but she didn't stop. She leaped and scrambled onto the ledge, disappearing into the hedges below. On the bed, Aengus heaved himself to standing. He didn't fall back down this time, but he did sway for a moment. He placed a hand on the foot board for support.

I opened my mouth to complain, but my words evaporated. Standing up at the same time in my tiny room had our proximity unbelievably close. My direct line of sight was his bare chest beneath the black trench coat. If I lifted my hand, I could do what he'd demanded I shouldn't — couldn't — and place my hand on his skin. My stomach fluttered at the thought. He claimed touch would hurt me, even kill me. How was that possible? And more importantly was he the villain or the hero?

And did it matter?

The list of unanswered questions was only growing. I wanted to tell him he had to stay and answer them, but that would mean I was literally demanding he stay in my bedroom.

Suddenly, even fully dressed in jeans and a pullover hoodie, I felt exposed.

What was wrong with me? I didn't drool over guys or girls. Sure, I could appreciate a beautiful person, but get hot and bothered, never. None of my few dates had ended in the bedroom.

I could handle my own needs, no need to add a stranger to the mix. Especially a stranger who might just find out how weird I really was. If they didn't already know, that is. I didn't let myself linger on the fact Aengus wouldn't be bothered by my life; his was just as bizarre.

I forced my attention away from his chest and up to his face. His golden eyes dilated as he stared into mine. A deep visceral pull twisted up through me. I couldn't look away. I didn't want to. Aengus leaned closer. Heat, like a summer bonfire, filled the space between us. It stole my breath.

His face hardened. "No. No. NO!" He whirled away from me and stumbled toward the door. The heat disappeared and the shock of its loss made me gasp. "Merlin was right," he admonished. "I am a fool. I have a duty to close the veil. To keep it closed. And yet, here I am, easily distracted by a pretty face."

Did he mean me? Was I the pretty face? Wait, did he say Merlin? "You can't just say the name Merlin and then storm out."

He paused and looked over his shoulder. "Stay here. I don't know why the *ossorians* have been sent after you, but once I have the sword it won't matter. I'll close the veil and all will be as it was." He yanked open the door and rushed out.

"What does any of that mean?" I yelled as I followed him out into the kitchen, but he was gone. I hadn't even heard the back door open or close. Gone, just like his disappearing act in the museum.

I took a deep breath before Aengus's last words registered. Once he had the sword? That jerk was going back to the museum to try again!

I rushed down the main hall toward the front entrance, hoping to cut Aengus off as he came around the house. Everett, monitoring the residents at his desk in the main room, raised an eyebrow at me. I never take the front entrance. "There's a bee flying around the back door," I lied.

"Bears now bees, I think mother nature has it out for you," he teased.

I forced a laugh. As I grabbed the door handle, the doorbell rang. I froze in surprise. The residents, including Mr. Friedman and Ms. Carlton, were watching television or playing cards. *Jeopardy* had given way to *Judge Judy*. They all turned toward the door and me. Everett stood up and strode past me to open it when it became obvious I wasn't going to.

On the other side of the storm door stood a stately woman, probably in her early fifties, with pristine hair and makeup in a slimming, deep green pant suit, and a large brown purse tucked up under her arm. At least, that's what Everett saw. What I saw, like a double image one on top of the other was a whole lot more terrifying.

The deep green was the color of her skin, clearly visible as she wore no clothes over her drooping breasts and a distended stomach. Her tendrils of black hair lay in clumps down her face, framing the narrow, pointed chin and hawklike nose between sunken cheeks. Under her arm was not a purse, but another head attached to her side, matching in appearance to the one sitting on her shoulders. Her arm curled under the chin and held it upright.

"Can I help you, ma'am?" Everett asked politely.

"Actually, I'm here to see the young lady behind you," the bog witch looking woman said, her voice clear and firm and at the same time rasping and mangled as both heads spoke.

Everett pushed the storm door open, but the bog witch only ran her eyes along the doorframe without taking a step forward. "That's alright. It will only be a moment. I just need a quick word with the young lady about a mutual Brownie friend."

Nibs had gone outside a moment ago. I rushed forward.

Everett turned to me with his hand on his chest in fake indignation. "You have a cookie dealer and you didn't share?"

I forced a laugh as I stepped outside. "Don't worry. I'll grab you a box of Thin Mints."

"And a Caramel Delight. Just don't tell my wife."

"Our little secret," I agreed.

Everett grinned and closed the storm door. Through the glass, I saw Mr. Friedman, from his recliner eyes wide, clearly seeing the danger. The bracelet. The *Sul Aos Si*. I worried Mr. Friedman would raise an alarm, which I was certain would just put him and the residents in harm's way. I grinned back at him like everything was super normal and even gave him a ridiculous thumbs up. I hoped he believed me as Everett shut the main door leaving me alone on the porch with *her*. I desperately needed to figure out what to do next before I ended up the main course on her gingerbread house dinner table.

Nibbleink's unmistakable shriek carried across the lawn. "Too tight, too tight!"

I looked out to the curb, where a long, dark four-door sedan sat parked. Next to it stood a very hulking man in a matching dark suit, wearing sunglasses and a communication earpiece. In his plate sized hands, he held Nibbleink out away from his body like she was radioactive.

"Hey," I called out and stepped forward.

The bog witch extended the arm not holding her head to halt me. "I wouldn't upset my trell. He's likely to squeeze too hard and we were told specifically to bring you and the Brownie to the queen alive. I'd hate to have to tell her it's your fault we failed."

I raised my hands in surrender. "Don't hurt her."

"We won't," the bog witch smiled. "That comes later."

Chapter Eight

At least I wasn't in the trunk.

Was there a silver lining to being kidnapped?

Out the window, the familiar mountain pass toward Virginia City almost glowed under the sun. The desert sand and sparse fall vegetation created hues of gold and bronze. Autumn is always gilded here. I let the landscape hypnotize me into calm. Because if I was going to figure out how to get back home I needed to be calm.

It hadn't worked yet.

The copper-looking bangle the bog witch had demanded I let her put on my wrist burned where it rested on my skin and I could already make out a ring of red irritation. I tried to pull it off, but I couldn't. "What is this?"

"A queen's glamour," the bog witch answered as if that was an explanation.

"Which is what, exactly?"

The bog witch gave a withering stare over the back of the seat. "The bracelet conceals you from all but the fae and can only be removed by the fae who placed it. Now be quiet."

Concealed from all but the fae? That meant even if I managed to get free, I wouldn't be able to flag down anyone heading back toward Carson. I'd have to hoof it. And I'd stupidly forgot to grab the phone off the desk when I went after Aengus. No one knew where I was going. Even Nibs couldn't tell anyone as she was currently pouting in my arms, sending daggers out her eyes at Trell and the bog witch in the front seat. When we'd first gotten in the car, Nibs had shaken her fist and let out a string of profanities, until the bog witch hissed "Silence" and Nibs was forced to just glare.

While we sat trapped, Nibs set aside her anger long enough to confirm that the two-headed fae was indeed a variety of bog witch, and Trell, apparently, was both his name and his race when I asked. I wanted more clarity, but the bog witch hushed us again.

The quiet in the car was broken again only when Trell touched a finger to his earpiece and said, "Confirmed." He took his eyes off the road for a brief moment to glance at the bog witch. "There's been word of a sighting about a mile ahead. We're to stop and investigate."

The bog witch huffed but nodded.

Dirt and gravel crunched beneath the wheels as we rolled to a stop alongside the highway. I looked out the window. A sighting of what? The only thing to break up the nothingness was sagebrush and a few cars passing in opposite directions. Again, the fact this was a kidnapping didn't escape me. Were they planning on killing me? No one would find me for ages out here. I'd be picked clean by scavengers. They'd need dental records to identify me. Panic had me yanking on the door latch. The child lock was on, but I only pulled on it harder. The plastic threatened to snap off in my grip.

"Enough," the bog witch snapped and I jumped, letting go of the handle. "You'll be safe in the car."

Safe? How would I be safe if they were going to "eighty-six" me — taking me eighty miles out and six feet deep? Granted that was more of a Vegas mob thing, but I wasn't putting it past these fae.

Trell looked over at the bog witch. "You should stay, too. I'll go."

"No. You know the queen will expect me to report," the bog witch said as they both opened their respective door and stepped out. Trell in his FBI looking suit and the bog witch bare, her greenish gray skin still looking damp even under the harsh sunlight, walked out into the desert. In the distance past them, just beyond clear sight, I thought I saw something rounded and covered in fur.

I set Nibs on the seat next to me and slid over the console into the front.

The keys were gone. Damn.

I quietly opened the car door. Nibs crawled over as well and reached for me. I picked her up and stuffed her in the hoodie pocket. She poked her head out with a smile.

I barely let the car door latch closed to avoid notice.

I was free.

Technically.

The sun baked the top of my head as I gazed down the road toward civilization. Where at the moment not even a car could be seen as it stretched out across the desert, nearly shimmering into invisibility. Not that anyone would notice me with the bracelet on. The logical part of me knew I'd never make it before I dehydrated, even in the fall, but I still had to fight the urge to start running toward town. "Let's see what's up," I told Nibs, turning away from the road. Even if I couldn't get to safety, more information was going to help me save myself. I hoped.

I made my way through the scrub brush, the sand heating the bottom of my shoes and warming my feet. A ground squirrel hole nearly took me out. I managed to stay upright only by grabbing onto a sagebrush. The sharp branches cut into the side of my palm. I inhaled sharply and shoved the cut up to my mouth. A few drops of blood stained the sand.

Ahead, both Trell and the bog witch had stopped. The furred lump viewed from the road now rose like a hillock in front of them.

I walked closer, still sucking on my wound. The bog witch turned in my direction, both faces irritated. "You don't listen to directions well," the top head said with a sneer.

Maybe following my kidnappers out into the desert was a bad idea. I ducked my head and looked away from her to the furry mound.

My stomach heaved as I noticed the smell. I dropped my hand from my mouth and gagged. Desperate to get away from the putrid rot, I held my sleeve against my nose. Flies buzzed in a swirling black cloud over the distended abdomen of a large mule deer baking in the sun. The chest had been ripped open, ribcage spread wide, and I wasn't a veterinarian but organs were definitely missing.

I was suddenly reminded of the picture of the mutilated horses Diana had shown me. Could whatever had killed the mustangs have killed the buck, too?

"Another has escaped," the bog witch remarked to Trell.

"Yes, ma'am," he answered.

I lowered my sleeve away from my face. "Escaped... like out of a cage? Do you have creatures that can do this just sitting in cages somewhere?"

The bog witch smirked with both black lips. "The *custos* used to take better care of their own." She sniffed in distaste and stomped toward me, her ponderous feet crushing the golden scrub as she walked. I thought for a moment she would grab me, but she made no move to as I stepped out of her way. She continued walking back to the car.

"*Custos?*" I wondered out loud. Aengus had used that word.

"In the past, anyone with fae blood would be raised by the *custos*. They would have trained you, given you knowledge about us." Trell explained.

"Like a school?"

Nibs giggled deep in the recess of my pocket.

Trell paused as if searching for the right word. "No, like an army, but once they closed the veil, the practice eventually dissolved."

All his words separately made sense, but altogether seemed like gibberish. "Closed the veil?"

"Your lack of knowledge is vast." His tone clearly implied it was a severe lack on my part.

If I had hackles they'd have been standing straight up. Indignation fed my words. "I have knowledge. I *know* I've been kidnapped. I *know* there's something killing animals and it isn't a normal predator." I pointed to the dead deer and tried not to breathe in too deeply. "And I *know* I can see things others can't. What I don't *know*, is why. And honestly, even if there was such a thing as this *custos* I wouldn't join. I just want to be left alone." My mouth snapped shut when I finished as I realized I'd said all that to my kidnapper.

Trell didn't look angry. His expression remained stoic as he said, "Being *custos* wasn't a choice."

"Well, then I'm definitely glad it's gone."

Trell raised an eyebrow.

The bog witch called from beside the car, "Come along, the Queen of the Unseelie Court does not appreciate being made to wait."

The Unseelie Court? Court as in knights and ladies and jousting? I'd gone to Tahoe once for a renaissance faire. They'd had a queen and her court who had walked down the middle of the vendors, making visitors scurry to the sides. Everyone was supposed to bow or curtsy. I hadn't known. I was the only one left upright. It was awkward. Nibs had used the term Unseelie and Seelie before, but not as a court, just as a descriptor for certain fae I'd come across. To be honest, the Unseelie fae had seemed a bit scarier.

And now I was being taken to their home base. I had spent my whole life avoiding the fae world and suddenly I had a guest spot in a large supernatural story with no idea what I was expected to do. And honestly, I was pretty sure nothing good would come of it.

I looked over my shoulder. Trell now stood with tree trunk legs spread and bulging arms folded across his chest. Human or not, if I ran he'd no doubt tackle me, and then I'd be right back where I was now but with more bruises and covered in dirt. Or he'd let me go and I'd die from the elements, or possibly be eaten by the same creature that had munched on the mule deer.

I returned to the car, Trell's heavy tread behind me, and resumed my seat in the back. Nibs crawled out of my pocket as I buckled. I had to hope the fae didn't want me dead. Fingers crossed. My nausea now was more about my lack of choices than putrid smell. If I vomited in the car, I wouldn't feel the least bit bad.

Chapter Nine

We rolled to a stop in an empty parking lot. A wooden sign stated, "Closed for the Season."

"A mine tour?"

Neither Trell nor the bog witch answered. Nibs poked her head out of my pocket, curled her lip in disgust, and disappeared.

The dark entrance to the mine stood open from the hillside, yawning like an earthen Venus fly trap waiting for its next victim. Like any self-respecting history nerd, I'd been up to Virginia City many times, and taken tours of houses, casinos, and graveyards, but mines? Deep underground with only old wood timbers holding back tons of body-crushing earth? No, I don't think so.

My palms itched with sweat and I scrubbed them against my jeans and hunched deeper into the seat. Trell opened my door and stared down. "You will come with us now."

"I'm n-n-not very comfortable going in there. You know, under all that dirt," I stammered.

The bog witch slammed her door shut. I watched through the windshield as she walked around the hood to stand by the pipe fencing surrounding the mine entrance. Power suit or naked with green skin, both ways she seemed out of place.

Trell reached into the car. Fearing he'd drag me out, I scurried underneath his hand and stepped out onto the pea gravel. He nodded with approval, then walked toward the bog witch. She had removed a lock and chain. Trell lifted the gate with little effort and dragged it across the dirt.

I reached the front of the car and stopped. How was I going to get out of this? My mind bounced from one idea to the next, but I couldn't think of anything that would work. I was stuck.

The bog witch eyed me with her four eyes as if I were a bug, one she wouldn't mind squishing under her heel. "This way," she called, and didn't wait to see if I followed.

If I didn't die today, it would be a miracle.

The air in Nevada is very dry. In the heat of summer, it can feel like you're being baked in an oven and in the winter the sharp wind will leach every bit of moisture from any exposed skin. I didn't go anywhere without lotion and lip balm. But only a few feet into the dark of the mine and I felt the cool moisture in the air. The smell of damp earth was almost overwhelming and the ground sucked at my shoes with every step.

I followed the bog witch, Trell bringing up the rear, as we made our way down the slow descending grade into the mountainside. Along the wall, barred yellow lights dimly lit the tunnel. My heart felt caged just like the little canaries the miners would bring into the deep to check the air quality as it tried to pound out of my chest.

The deeper we walked, the more the ceiling seemed to press downward. I could barely take a full breath. Each step was a challenge. I tried not to think about cave ins or dying canaries. Only the hulking form of Trell stomping behind me kept me moving forward.

"Nibs," I whispered. She poked her head out and looked

around warily. "Didn't you say fae hated iron? This mountain is chock full of it. Why would a court be here?"

She screwed up her face in confusion. "Natural in mountain. Not formed by humans." She dropped back into the pocket without any further explanation. So much for trying to keep my mind off imminent death.

The bog witch turned down a much older and less maintained part of the mine. I stopped right before stepping under the bowing wooden lintel. Trell's massive form pressed into my space without even touching me. I looked over my shoulder hoping to catch a glimpse of open sky at the mine entrance, but my whole vision was filled up by 'secret service' black.

"If you don't walk, Trell will carry you," the bog witch called as she continued further into the shadowed shaft.

I faced the gloom and glanced up one more time at the dipping wood beam. With a deep breath, I ducked my head, hunched my shoulders and stepped forward.

Farther in, a lantern glowed an unnatural blue, weakly pushing back at the shadows. Part of me wished for more light, but then I'd be able to see the low ceilings and crumbling walls and that seemed worse than the dark.

The deeper we went the cooler it got. I shivered and pulled my arms in tight. Finally, the bog witch stopped. Another of the glowing blue lanterns illuminated large double doors depicting reveling fae creatures of all types. Black lightning like scars arched across the carvings from every direction. The entrance should have fronted a large gothic mansion and not a dirt wall. And yet there it stood. The bog witch reached out and tapped her fist on one side. Both doors swung open on silent hinges. She gestured for me to enter first.

Into the Unseelie Court.

Staring into the spacious and vaulted room my fear of what the fae could do to me paled in comparison to the claustrophobic mine shaft. I immediately crossed the threshold into pastels and gold. The ceilings reached a good fifteen, maybe even twenty, feet high. Large palm frond plants in gilded pots were spaced equidistance along the walls. How were they even alive without sun? Gold framed mirrors hung on robin's egg blue walls with white wainscotting. Gone was the wet damp of dirt, now smothered by the cloying scent of potpourri. Couches and armchairs, in floral patterns filled the areas on either side of a mauve runner leading to a wide dais directly in front of us. The dais had three wooden steps stretching the length and on top it held an empty wicker throne with an expansive fan backrest.

Either the queen loved the '80s, or she'd never left it.

Aside from the outdated décor, the room was empty.

Nibs poked her head out, sighed deeply, before disappearing back inside the pocket.

"Keep moving," the bog witch demanded. I startled, realizing I was gaping, and sped up. The bog witch and Trell followed close behind.

Bells like singing glass tinkled from every direction, as large sections of the walls opened inwards revealing themselves to be doors. Fae started to enter the room. Their whispers and murmurs created a low hum as they took a seat or hovered behind the couches and chairs. None of them were glamoured. None of them looked human. Large and small. Horned and scaled. Spiked and furred. There were so many different terrifying variations.

My fear expanded until it exploded through me, leaving me numb.

I watched everything around me with detachment.

That was probably a bad thing, but not feeling panic allowed me to notice the relief that also appeared. I never realized how much mental energy I had given to appearing normal. Talking with strangers was like carefully traversing steppingstones across a creek, each word requiring a steady and balanced step. A slow progression of stutters and restarts to keep myself from falling. Now standing in the Unseelie Court, despite the uncertainty, the enormous weight of constant control lifted.

Behind the wicker throne, another wall section opened and a human looking woman emerged in a blue sequin, floor length gown and blonde hair teased toward the ceiling like a rodeo queen. Her makeup was bright and garish with almost neon pink blush and blue eye shadow. She was glamoured, but unlike every fae I'd seen before, her true self was hidden. Only when she moved was there a slight wobble in her mask, but it didn't drop enough for me to see beneath. Every nerve in my body cried "danger," She gracefully lowered and perched on the edge of the wicker throne.

The room was immediately silenced.

For the second time today, I felt underdressed in jeans and a pullover hoodie. I also didn't think she would appreciate the ironic phrase across the front: I Believe in Magic. Sometimes humor is the only way to make the most of a crappy situation.

Behind the queen stood a massive fae, a wall of moving plant life, with vine corded arms and legs. They towered over the queen, clearly her guard. Boulder sized hands held what looked like a young tree capped with an ivory axe blade over their shoulder and the foliage knotted and twisted into shapes resembling a full suit of armor.

The bog witch laid a hand on my shoulder, her jagged black fingernails biting into my skin through the fabric. I squeaked, barely keeping myself from screaming. She pointed to the small lump in my hoodie pocket that was Nibbleink and motioned me to put her down.

"Nibs," I whispered. "They want you to come out."

"No," was her muffled reply.

I looked askance at the bog witch, who gestured again for Nibs to come out. "I don't think that's an option," I said opening one side of the pocket wider. Nibs, head low, crawled out and down my leg. When she reached the mauve carpet runner she refused to move away and held onto the fabric of my pants tightly.

"You will pay reverence to our queen, Saoirse," the bog witch commanded.

I wasn't sure if she meant I needed to bow, or curtsy, or prostrate myself on the floor. When her clawed finger poked into my back, I threw myself into a bow. I had to reach out to touch the mauve carpet to keep from falling on my face. Beside me, Nibs blinked, then, dressed in her overalls and scarf, demonstrated a perfect curtsy. Murmurs raced around the hall. If the bow was a bad choice, I couldn't change it now. What's done was done.

I straightened. The queen stared intently at me, saying nothing, her gaze burrowing through me. A bit of my earlier panic returned and my heart stuttered against my chest. Her eyes, ice blue and piercing, raked over me. Slowly, her gaze dropped.

"Nibbleink. Sweetheart. We were concerned when you left without permission." The queen's words were cordial, and her bright tone gave the allusion of concern, but there was an underlining scornfulness that added to my earlier opinion that the Unseelie queen was dangerous.

And what did she mean, left without permission? Left from the Unseelie Court? But Nibs said my father sent her. Was my father here? Was he fae? I couldn't help looking in all directions even though I had no idea what he looked like.

Saoirse snapped her fingers and Trell pressed forward from behind us. She pointed a long finger at Nibs. "Take the Brownie to her clan. We're sure they've been just as worried." Trell bent and ripped Nibs from my pantleg. "Don't forget to tell them we'll visit very soon." All pretense of brightness left the queen's voice.

"Wait!" I called, but Trell, with Nibs in hand, disappeared behind a wall door before I could utter another word.

Saoirse turned attention to the bog witch and smiled wide. "Those witches didn't give you any trouble, did they?"

The bog witch stepped to my side. "None, your majesty." She dipped her heads, before stepping back.

"Wonderful news. Now remove my glamour from the girl and

then go see if you can find Mistress Crone. Let her know we'd love to have her join us."

The bog witch nodded. She snatched up my arm and yanked the bracelet free. I rubbed my wrist and watched as she left through the same door as Trell and Nibs had used.

How had fae, living literally underground, know the retirement home residents were a coven and I hadn't? And I lived under the same roof! I was beginning to think I needed to pay more attention.

Saoirse noted my surprise. "Silly goose, of course we're aware of the coven hiding in plain sight protecting the little half breed." The queen, and her royal We, wrinkled her nose like she'd smelled something foul. Half breed? Did she mean me? "We choose to ignore. Besides, what do we care?" She waved her hand before her face. "The *custos* is no more and so is their power over us." She clapped like a child promised a new toy. "But tell us about the sword that has arrived in your place of employment. This sword found in a tomb."

"What are you going to do to Nibs?" I asked, ignoring her question. The queen stood up and loomed closer. Her smile was anything but nice.

"Don't worry about the Brownie, dear, we'll handle her soon. What we need to know is if Mistress Crone was correct. Is there such a sword?" Menace hung behind every saccharine-filled word spoken. She lowered herself to the seat.

"Technically," I managed to answer.

Saoirse frowned, her neon pink lips pressed together and one of her long fingernails clicked the wicker of the armrest. "What do you mean by technically?"

I froze. I didn't want to tell her anything. I wanted to get Nibs and get out of there. I might have for the briefest moment enjoyed the fact that I didn't have to pretend, but I wasn't fool enough to trade safety for a lack of disassembling.

The queen's gaze intensified. "We understand this is a bit overwhelming, but... " She shrugged and lifted a finger, mimicking running it down my cheek. She was quite a distance from me, yet I could feel the nail dig into my skin. I slapped my hand to my face where I had felt her touch more out of surprise than pain. "We don't really care." For a brief moment, her glamour dropped and I glimpsed the horrifying visage beneath.

My words tumbled out. "There was a sword, but there was this guy. And I tried to stop him, but your bog witch kidnapped me."

"Tried to stop him from what?" Saoirse asked. When I hesitated, she motioned more dramatically with her finger. Instead of a touch a sharp burn raced over my skin.

"From stealing it," I squeaked, as I touched the mark. Blood came away on my fingers.

Behind the throne, the Green Knight transferred the axe from one hand to the other. Saoirse leaned forward. "Did this sword thief have a name?"

"He didn't say." I answered quickly to keep her from using her magic to scratch me again. Aengus was a stranger and a thief, but he had saved me. It didn't feel right giving his name.

"Lie!" the knight boomed.

I jumped and Saoirse giggled. "Just like a *custos*. Never using the brains the fae gave them. If you lie, my knight will know and we'll be forced to extract the name by more forceful means." She was trying for a sympathetic tone. Why did she get to lie and I didn't?

And what was more forceful?

My mind spun in a circle, repeating "forceful means" over and over. I locked eyes with the queen. I clenched my jaw. I really didn't want to tell her.

She sighed heavily.

She reached out her hand in the air like a grappling hook. I felt the queen's fingers press against my chest, the nails boring their way into my skin. It didn't hurt, or more accurately the pain was covered by an intense desire to answer. I fought the urge, but it was impossible. Her magic pulled the word out of me. "Aengus," I mumbled.

The hall erupted in voices.

Saoirse dropped her hand and I fell to my knees. I rubbed at my chest and glared. Anger filled me where only fear had existed moments before as I pushed back up to standing. Around me some of the fae had shifted and formed groups, their conversations blending into a cacophony. One fae, dark and spider-like, skittered close to the carpet on its eight legs. I shrank away. It had four thin, articulated arms and its pale face held three eyes red as jewels over a slit-like mouth, which opened for a moment showing clicking pincers. The only clothing the fae wore was a kilt that wound around its human-like grey torso and draped over one shoulder. The spider fae winked one of its three red eyes at me.

"Silence, my darlings!" Saoirse commanded, and all murmurs and whispers immediately ceased. The queen turned to the knight behind her. "Bring me that sword and the Seelie puppet."

The eagerness in the way she said "seelie puppet" was unmistakable. After what the queen had just done to me I was hoping Aengus had already stolen the sword. At this point, Aengus was definitely the lesser of the two evils.

The vines and foliage of the Green Knight's body creaked and rustled as they stepped down off the dais, scattering the fae. The doors opened as they neared, and they bent under the lintel and disappeared out into the mine. The doors shut without a sound behind them.

I turned back to face the queen. She sat deeper on her throne, the fan back matching her halo of big hair. Saoirse snapped her fingers and called out, "Dennriall, you're late."

The Spider fae — Dennriall — stepped forward. "Apologies, I was detained."

The queen seemed to contemplate making him explain further, but then pointed to me. "We're curious. We want to know who would sully themselves with a human after all this time." She scrunched her nose up. The "eew" was implied. "We are finally free of those meddling *custos*, and we won't allow the practice to resume."

Dennriall nodded to the queen and then turned to face me. The pincers in his open mouth clicked and his jeweled eyes were focused and unblinking. I thought of Nibs and fought the urge to take a step back. If I died, who would save her? "Give me your hand," he said, his voice surprisingly deep and gentle. But I looked at him with suspicion. He winked one of his eyes again. I couldn't tell if it was tick, or if it meant something. "I won't harm you. Give me your hand," he assured me.

As if I had a choice. I could obviously be made to do whatever the queen wanted. I clenched my fist and stretched out my arm. Dennriall took my hand in two of his four. The carapace along his fingers felt sharp and cold against my skin. Before I could pull away, he dropped his head over my wrist and the pincers in his mouth stabbed into my skin. "Ow," I screeched and yanked my wrist free. "You said you wouldn't harm me." Blood welled over the two small puncture marks.

"You are unharmed. My bite was without venom. Now if you would let me continue, I can answer the queen's question. Give me your hand." The surrounding fae had crowded close. Dennriall ordered everyone to step back and give me space. Maybe he really didn't want to harm me, but as I reached out, my hand trembled. Fae caused harm, that's what they did.

Dennriall pulled my arm close and bent over it. I tried not to gag when he licked the blood off my skin. So gross. The spider fae hummed. He looked up, his eyes glowed for a second before fading back to their normal jewel like glint. He swiftly raised my other hand and urged me to put pressure on the bite before he turned to the queen.

"She has fae blood, there is no doubt, but the lineage is muddled. It may be too diluted by human blood to know which fae dabbled, your highness." Dennriall said bowing his head.

Saoirse twisted her mouth in irritation. "Fine, it doesn't matter." She stood up and adjusted her dress, the sequins flashing like tiny stars. "Dennriall, find a nice place for our guest. We'll decide what to do with it later." I knew Saoirse's definition of guest differed from mine greatly. Cold, hard fingers tightened around my arm and I tried to rip free. What to do with me? Screw this! I needed to find Nibs and get the hell out of this time warp and away from the fae. But Dennriall's grip remained firm on my wrist.

"Don't resist," he snapped under his breath. "It will only cause you more pain." Anger, sharp and swift coursed through me and I envisioned myself kicking out one of the spider fae's knees. I'd show him pain.

Maybe I could convince the queen I didn't have any more use and then maybe she'd just let me go. Or she'd kill me. Was it worth the gamble? I glanced at the dais, but the queen was already gone, the door in the wall clicking shut behind her.

I sagged. "I need to get out of here," I whined.

"That's good, because I want to help you," Dennriall said yanking on my arm, leading me into the crowd.

Chapter Ten

I pulled to a stop amidst the crowd. Dennriall looked over his shoulder to me but didn't release my wrist.

"The fae don't just help, not without payment." If I'd been less shocked, I might have thought of something less rude to say to a potential ally, but I lived this every day with Nibs. If I wanted something from her, I had to pay up. No way was he trying to help out of the kindness of his heart.

Dennriall pinched his slit-like mouth until the skin wrinkled in protest. He glanced over his shoulder at the surrounding fae who were chatting and talking amongst themselves now that the queen was gone. When he looked back at me, he sighed dramatically. "Not you personally, but I am in your father's debt, and since I cannot repay him, helping you should be enough."

"You know my father?" Disbelief quickly turned to curiosity.

Dennriall took a long pause before nodding.

"Can you tell me where he is? Or at least give me a name? Anything?" A loud, raucous group of fae descended around us. A towering fae with large breasts and tiny horns peeking through her wild dark hair smiled seductively in my direction. Dennriall pulled hard on my wrist and I stumbled after him.

"We must go now," he urged. "Follow me."

A fae dressed in a wide tutu and carrying a tray of hors d'oeuvres glided near. They slid the tray out to me and I could smell the savory cheese and meats. I lifted a hand and the fae server pushed the tray closer. "And don't eat or drink anything!" Dennriall snapped.

I jumped and turned away from the food. My stomach grumbled in protest. When had I eaten last?

Cautiously optimistic I might survive, I followed without complaint as we wove our way through the hall around furniture and mingling fae. A minotaur-like fae with long wide horns leaned in close as I passed and sniffed deeply, his nostrils wet and flaring near my face. I ducked only to nearly run into a fae with a mouth stretching the length of their very wide face, teeth sharp and gleaming. Dennriall continued to pull me along, keeping me from melting to the floor in fear.

We broke through one last group of fae and found ourselves in front of a wall. Dennriall set his hand along the wainscotting. I didn't see a button or a lever, but at his touch the section opened inward. The spider fae pulled me through the opening and the wall closed seamlessly behind us.

What looked like an endless corridor stretched out on either side. The décor displayed more of the same from the larger hall — robin's egg blues and golds. On the surface it looked harmless but gone was the smell of potpourri replaced with mold and stagnant water and now I felt the damp of the mine. The walls rippled at the corner of my eyes. Nothing was as it seemed.

Dennriall had not let go of my wrist and tried to tug me along. The bite he'd made earlier stung and I twisted my hand trying to get free. He looked over his double shoulder, his slit like mouth pinched tight again, but he let my wrist go. "You are not safe here. We must go. Quickly."

I scrutinized the red and irritated bite. "Was it true you don't know who my fae ancestor is?" I asked.

He looked both ways down the hall, then pinned me with his tri-jeweled stare. "There is no mistaking that taste. You must understand, the queen would not have dismissed you so hastily if she had known. Or left you without proper guards."

"What am I?"

"You are royalty." Dennriall paused and took a deep breath. "And you are dangerous."

Royalty? Dangerous? "Yeah, I seriously doubt that," I said, rolling my eyes.

"You do not have to believe a thing for it to be real. Now please, we must hurry."

When he grabbed on and yanked again, my legs finally moved. The hallway remained empty as we sped down it. There were corridors branching off from the main hall that had not been noticeable at first. We turned left when the corridor branched the first time, then left again, and another left.

"I didn't think the fae could lie, but you told the queen you couldn't taste who my relatives were," I questioned as we ran.

"Fae can lie," he answered. "But our magic knows the truth. We cannot lie to ourselves so out of habit we rarely do. And I didn't say couldn't. I said it was complex. And it is."

At a block of wall that looked the same as any other part of the corridor, Dennriall stopped. With a touch of his hand, the wall opened into a tiny circular sitting room. A large tapestry with a scene of a walled garden and bench covered one side. The only furniture was a small round table and two delicate, ornate chairs padded in aqua cushions.

"Wait here," Dennriall commanded gesturing me to enter. "I need to find a working portal to send you from Underhill."

"Underhill? I thought this was the Unseelie Court?"

"I don't have time to explain the complexities of our world. Just stay here and stay quiet," Dennriall responded, clearly irritated.

I refused. It was bad enough I was trusting a fae on the flimsy knowledge he knew my father. I wasn't about to leave without Nibs. "What about Nibbleink?"

"What?"

"My friend who came with me. I can't leave without her."

"The Brownie," Dennriall sighed deeply and looked skyward in frustration.

I crossed my arms. "I won't leave without her."

Dennriall dipped his torso so his face was even with mine. "The longer you stay, the harder it will be for me to get you out."

I stared, unblinking. "Not without Nibbleink."

He clicked his pincers in obvious frustration. "Fine. I will locate your Brownie. Now please stay here until I return. Your father may *owe* me when this is over and done with." It was the best assurance I was going to get. I stepped into the tiny room. He skittered back and closed the door.

Immediately I tried the latch. It opened easily. Not a prisoner. That was a relief. I leaned out into the hallway. Dennriall was nowhere in sight. I pulled my head back into the room. Hopefully I wouldn't have to wait too long for his return.

"You're the mongrel brought in today?" a feminine voice said behind me. "What luck."

I screamed, spinning around and falling hard against the closed door.

I'd been certain the room was empty, but now a fae woman sat in one of the chairs. Long white hair framed a narrow face so pale it was hard to tell where her skin stopped and her white floor-length gown began. She looked like a marble statue given life. Only her dark eyes broke the illusion. One side of her bloodless lips raised in what could have been a smile or a snarl. The background smell of mold and stagnant water seemed to intensify.

Instinct screamed for me to run. My eyes still trained on the fae, I reached behind me and fumbled for the door latch. She languidly raised her hand and twisted her wrist as if to snatch something in front of her. The air instantly thickened around me. A weight settled onto my shoulders and chest, pushing my arms to my sides. I couldn't move. I could barely draw a breath and the pounding of my heart threatened to take the last of it.

The fae stood and moved toward me. Each step flowed into the next like she floated rather than walked through the space. Inches from me, she ran a finger over the injury on my cheek. It burned hot and cold. I wanted to stop her, but I could only twitch my fingers uselessly.

"You're not what was promised," she said and I clearly heard the disappointment in her voice. She reached out and grabbed the wrist Dennriall had bitten. A burning cold raced up my arm. My outcry never left my chest. "Hmmm, the seneschal has tasted you. We will need to speak, he and I." She dropped my arm and eyed me, her head cocked to the side. "What is your name?"

I gaped like a fish until she made the same motion she'd made earlier. The weight smothering me immediately disappeared. I fumbled for the door latch, but the fae raised her hand threateningly and I stopped.

"Your name," she asked again.

Nibs had said once that names have power. No way was I handing this fae any more power over me. I grabbed the first name I could think of — my mother's. "Mira," I answered.

"Mira," the fae repeated. She looked like she wanted to say something more but stopped. Her gaze seemed to pierce through the wall. "The seneschal returns. I will find you again," she said, her words clipped with irritation. In the next instant, she burst into a fog, bits of ice pelleting the walls and me, and was gone.

Shocked, it took me a minute to move when the door behind me tried to open. I finally stepped aside when Dennriall demanded if I was alright.

The spider fae skittered in holding Nibs in the crook of one of his arms. They'd taken all of her doll clothes. She was bare. Of course, I'd found her that way when we'd first met, but her fashion had become such an integral part of her personality it was unnerving to see her without anything on. "Nibs, are you okay?" I asked. Roughly, Dennriall pushed Nibs into my arms.

"They took my clothes," she screeched with indignation. She grabbed a fistful of my sweatshirt. "I am rage."

Dennriall pulled out a hidden dagger. For a brief second, I feared what he would do with it, but he pulled the draped kilt from his shoulder and cut a strip from the hem. He handed the piece of cloth to Nibs. Anger gone in an instant, Nibs grinned. With nimble fingers, she tied the piece of cloth like a sarong. She twisted and twirled, admiring her new outfit.

Dennriall returned his dagger to its hidden location and readjusted his kilt. "We have only minutes before Trell recovers and finds your Brownie missing. We must go now." He clicked his pincers for good measure.

I encouraged Nibs to crawl into my hoodie pocket for easy transport. She didn't argue.

"Quickly." He picked up his pace until we were running across the velvet runner. Even though we turned right out of the room and logic dictated we'd need to take another right, there was no cross hallway. We ran straight up to the wall, that held a closed door. The first actual door I'd seen.

"This doesn't make any sense," I whispered out loud.

Dennriall huffed. "Underhill never does. This door will take you to one of our fae establishments. I'm sorry I don't know which one. This exit is a rush, but it will take you out of the court and back into the human world."

I looked to the door and then at Dennriall. "Do you think the queen will send the *ossorians* after me again?"

Dennriall straightened, his legs lifting his torso higher. "*Ossorians* haven't existed since the veil was closed. How do you know of them?"

I wanted to tell him they very much existed, but I could sense the topic was one we didn't have time to discuss. But if Dennriall didn't know about last night's attack, it was likely the Unseelie Court hadn't sent them. I shrugged. "Probably mixed up what I saw with a name I read in a book."

Dennriall lowered slightly and I took that for a good sign.

I set my hand on the knob and paused. "Th—" I started to say just as Nibs jabbed an elbow into my stomach from the pocket. "Ow, Nibs, what the hell?"

"Your Brownie is right. Do not thank the fae. You do not want to be in our debt."

"Okay, I won't," I said. How could I have forgotten the number one rule Nibs had told me about the fae? But I still couldn't go. I could tell Dennriall had risked a lot to help, but I wondered if I could get one more thing before I went through the door. "My father, you must know his name. Could you tell me, please?"

"Stubborn human." He looked over his shoulder. Somewhere near, I heard the sounds of stomping feet. He looked back at me. Did I imagine sadness in his jeweled eyes? "Your father was stubborn, too. Now go."

A group of militarily dressed behemoths, their spiked helmeted heads nearly brushing the ceiling, rounded a corner. I knew I should go, but this might be the only time I could learn anything. "His name? Please."

"Geoffrey Corben. Now you must go!"

With my father's name ringing in my ears, I fell through the open doorway into the stall of a public bathroom.

Chapter Eleven

With Nibs still hidden in my hoodie pocket and my father's name repeating in my mind, I stepped out of the restroom—into the Nugget Casino. The replica old-school Batmobile was a dead giveaway.

The last time I'd entered this particular casino was on a date in high school. The boy had wanted to get burgers and insisted that the old Nevada ambiance was key to a good burger. It was lost on me. All the servers and most of the patrons had been fae. I spent the entire meal convinced they'd realize I could see through their glamour and drag me away. To where? I had no idea, but somewhere bad, I was certain.

And after what just happened at the Unseelie Court, I think my fears were warranted.

I don't remember much about the boy or what was said that night. He never asked me out again, which was fine by me, and I spent the entire next day curled up in my bed. I do remember Grandpa coming in and giving me a nip of his whiskey and warning me to steer clear of the Nugget. Not about gambling. With slot machines in every grocery store and mini mart, the shine rubs off pretty quickly. No, because he didn't know why or how but the Nugget catered to the fae.

I hadn't stepped foot into the Nugget since.

Until today.

Grandpa's warnings screamed in my head as I flipped up my hood, not caring if it looked suspicious. I didn't want to see any more fae. The Unseelie Court had given me enough nightmare fuel. I could admit, as far as fae went, Dennriall was at the very least not so bad, but I stopped myself from thinking about what could have happened if he hadn't sent me through the doorway. I just wanted to get home. Grandpa had been right to urge me to stay away from the fae. I needed to follow that advice. Now more than ever.

Luckily, the casino seemed mostly empty, just a few hunched figures gambling further into the slots, mostly fae with a few humans sprinkled in. A shroud of decades-old cigarette smoke hung in the air. Head down, I followed the circles and diamond pattern of the stiff piled carpet, looking up only briefly to orient myself. The ringing and dinging of the slot machines drowned out the overhead music, creating a cacophony of desperation. A few feet ahead, sunlight overrode the halogen lighting and knew I was almost out. I picked up my pace.

I raised my head as I neared the door. My field of vision was completely filled with someone heading in the opposite direction. It took me a moment to realize it was Aengus, still missing a shirt, his attention elsewhere. I only had time to raise my hands as a shield before we collided. My palms rested on warm hard muscle and then the world went black.

I had no sense of how much time had passed before sound, warped and fuzzy, slowly materialized out of the darkness.

"What did you do?" I heard Nibs question, her voice a squeaky growl.

"She only touched me for a moment. There should be no ill effects." I recognized Aengus' voice above me.

"Why isn't she awake?" Clearly Nibs did not believe him. Aengus must have moved closer because Nibs demanded he stay back.

My little protector might take things a bit too far. I needed to open my eyes and let her know I was okay. At least, I thought I was. With great effort, I worked my heavy lids open and saw Nibs standing at attention on my chest.

"I'm fine," I croaked. I blinked a few times as I turned my head and found my entire view filled with bare chest beneath an open long coat. The bandages were gone. Perfectly smooth skin existed where Aengus had been horribly injured only last night. If not for the dried blood flaking off his skin, I'd question my sanity.

Oh no. How long had I been staring at his chest? I squeezed my eyes shut.

"She's passed out again," Nibs squeaked. "And she's all red. What did you do?" I could feel her little hands patting my cheeks.

"No, no, I'm fine." I opened my eyes making sure not to look in Aengus's direction. Nibs' nose was nearly pressed up against mine and her black eyes were large with concern. "I'm fine," I assured her again. Was I fine? Prepared this time, I turned my head toward Aengus, looking up past his chest to his face. "I'm fine, right?" I asked.

"Yes, almost certainly," he assured me.

I tried not to let the "almost" bother me. "What was that?" I lifted Nibs off and tried to sit up. My head swam for a moment, threatening to take me under again, but I stayed upright.

"By *that* you mean my touch causing you to swoon?"

I scowled at the term. I remembered trying to help him remove his coat in the kitchen and now his reaction made more sense. "How is that even possible?"

Aengus stood up from his crouch. He turned away, his jaw hardened. "The fae have ways to alter a human. Like the *ossorian*."

There was something infinitely worse than the fact fae could not just injure humans, but actually alter their very being. "They turn humans into beasts?"

Aengus stared at the bright afternoon light coming through the casino doors. "Yes."

"But you look human. I mean, you're not all over hairy or anything."

He looked back down at me. "No, I'm not an *ossorian*. I'm *fola tráill*. The slave of the blood."

"Blood? Like a vampire? But I just touched you. You didn't drink my blood. Wait, you didn't, right?" I patted my neck for wounds.

He unclenched his jaw with a short laugh. "The vampire part is as good a description as any, but Merlin altered me, and now I drain life and magic by touch." He spoke like his words were inconsequential, but his eyes looked sad.

Before I could wrap my head around the fact that this was the second time he'd mentioned the name Merlin, the hostess from the diner rushed across the casino floor. "Miss, are you unwell?" she called, her voice like that of a lifetime smoker. Outwardly, she appeared as an older lady with a bad perm and large glasses on a beaded chain. Beneath the glamour, she was also a squatty orcish woman with grey skin. Oddly, the two parts seemed to match up well. She stopped abruptly when she noticed Aengus. Her demeanor turned cold. "We don't serve your kind." All her concern had disappeared.

Aengus tensed, but his tone remained even. "This is neutral territory."

She huffed and crossed her arms. "It doesn't mean livestock are welcome."

"I need no welcome, but I am meeting a prince of Seelie who would not be pleased that I was forced to leave."

The hostess's eyes narrowed. "You've made your point. How can I be of service?" She ground out the words in irritation.

"Just a quick repast for my friend."

I opened my mouth to disagree. There was no way I wanted to stay, but Aengus looked down at me. "In truth, that small touch should not have made you insensible. You must eat, or you may swoon again."

Before I could demand he stop using that word, my stomach rumbled. The last time I could remember eating was a midnight snack while Aengus had been passed out across my bed. I patted my pocket for my phone before remembering I still didn't have it. But it didn't really matter what time it was, it was definitely too many hours since I'd eaten.

Aengus pushed his coat to the side and pulled out his leather gloves that were folded over his belt, giving full view to the rusted and corroded sword hanging down his leg.

"You really did steal it." I don't think I quite believed he would go through with it.

"Again," he said, as he roughly tugged on his gloves, "I was not stealing. I was retrieving what was stolen *from* me." He reached down with a motion to indicate I should grab his hand to be helped up. I just stared at him.

"But they found it in a tomb. How is it yours?"

He gripped the hilt tightly in his other hand. Flecks of rust sprinkled to floor. "Because it was my tomb," he growled.

I remembered the article from earlier. "You're the Guardian, Beloved of the Dux?"

Aengus gave a self-depreciating laugh. "Beloved of the Dux? Hardly. I stood by Arthur only because of Gwynevere."

Excalibur. Merlin. Arthur. And now Gwynevere. Aengus spoke their names as if they really existed and weren't just stories. Despite my life already being filled with the unbelievable, my mind reeled. How was it I could accept fae lived among us, but the possibility that the legend of King Arthur and his Knights was real was too much? But if the legends were true, who was Aengus in all of this?

"Are you like Lancelot?" I asked as I stared up at him in confusion, but also curiosity.

Aengus scowled. "That was never my name." He motioned again for me to grab his hand.

Making sure to only touch the leather of the glove, I was shocked to find how warm his palm was even through the material. Weren't vampires supposed to be cold? I gained my feet and swayed. Nibs braced my calf as if she would be able to hold me up, but Aengus gripped my arm which did steady me. I nodded to let him know I wouldn't fall and he let go. Slowly.

"This way," the diner host called from across the casino, two large, laminated menus in her hand. She must have gone to fetch them while Aengus told me he was a fictional character come to life. I bent down and lifted Nibs and then we made our way toward the diner.

The host sat us in a booth in the very back corner away from most of the patrons, all fae, and forcefully slapped down the menus. "What do you wanna drink?"

We both asked for water. She snorted and stomped away.

Nibs crawled onto the table and started to pull out all the sugar packets, creating a pink and white fortification in front of her. She crossed her legs and sat in the middle. She grabbed one off the top and began to rip it open, then tipped her head back and poured the sugar into her open mouth.

Convinced Nibs was occupied for the next few minutes, at least, I turned my attention to Aengus. "Okay," I started.

Aengus raised an eyebrow and leaned against the back of the booth, crossing his arms.

"Say I believe you're a vampire and Lancelot." His eyes narrowed. "Fine, that you're Aengus whom the *character* of Lancelot was based on." He nodded. "But none of that's in the legends. There weren't vampires in those stories. King Arthur was supposed to be buried with the sword to rise again. He's the once and future king, not his best knight who had sex with his wife and caused the destruction of Camelot."

Aengus straightened and slammed a hand to the table. "Have sex with Gwynevere? Are you mad? She was like a sister." The disgust on his face looked genuine.

I winced. "To be fair, that part did always seem patriarchal, but everything else. The story doesn't match up."

A server arrived at our table and set down two ice waters. He was glamoured to look like a young college age guy with close cropped hair and dimples. That was not what he looked like underneath. I glanced his way and forced myself not to shudder as I focused on the menu. Remembering I didn't have my phone or wallet, I looked at Aengus. "I don't have a way to pay for food. We should go." I closed the menu and glanced at the server to apologize, my embarrassment overriding my fear. Aengus pulled a hundred dollar bill from within his jacket and set it on the table.

"Order," he said firmly. I blinked. "Please," he added more gently. I quickly ordered a french onion soup. Aengus ordered a bowl of fruit. Nibs just wanted to eat the sugar. We didn't argue. The server took the menus and left.

I rubbed a finger over the lip of my sweating glass of water. Part of me wanted to ask if he'd stolen the money too, but I knew how he would just go off again about not stealing the sword. Which he clearly did. I decided I didn't need to know about the money.

Aengus surveyed the diner and I remembered he'd said he was meeting a Prince of the Seelie. Barely escaping the Unseelie Court, I wasn't excited about meeting fae from the other court, even if Nibs categorized the Seelie as the "bossy ones who like laws." But my stomach growled again and I knew I'd never make it home if I didn't stay and eat. I'd have to hope I was safe for the time being.

Silence sat heavy between us. I noticed, but wouldn't let myself acknowledge, the return of the feeling I'd first experienced in the Unseelie Court. The feeling that everything was easier knowing I was surrounded by the fae. No hiding. No pretending.

"You ordered food. Does that mean you can eat?" I asked distracting myself from my thoughts.

Aengus stopped searching and looked at me. "Yes, I still need food."

"You said the fae made you a vampire, a *fola tráill*, then Merlin changed you, why? Why not just turn you back to human?"

Aengus looked confused by my question. "Because I needed to use Excalibur to close the veil to Innisfail."

Trell had talked about something getting through the veil, something that had mutilated the mule deer. But what was Innisfail? "I don't understand," I admitted.

Aengus furrowed his brow. "Maybe it is better that way."

Maybe he was right and I should just eat my soup and go home, but I bristled at being kept in the dark after finding out how much had been hidden from me by my grandpa. "I'd rather know."

He dipped his head in acquiescence. "Simply, as long as the sword and I both remained connected through Underhill to the earth and Innisfail, the veil between the realms was effectively locked. When my tomb was found and the sword taken, the lock failed and the veil opened." Aengus pulled his coat wide enough I could see the handle of the stolen sword. He looked down at it in frustration. "And now she is blocked from me, my connection to Excalibur appears broken and if that is true, I cannot close the veil again." He looked up stricken.

"And closing the veil last time meant being buried alive? And if you can fix Excalibur your plan is to, what, be buried alive, again?"

"I was never meant to wake up."

I shuddered at the thought of lying in a dark tomb. "Well, that seems like a shitty plan."

He laughed. "Merlin gave me one small mercy. It hurt him to do it, but Gwynevere insisted. My dreams were of the changing world. I saw the centuries come and go as I slept. But I must say, I have enjoyed experiencing this new world more than just dreaming of it."

"That explains why you're not freaking out about the cars and planes and things." I had wondered how someone from medieval Britain seemed so chill.

Aengus sat back against the booth again. "I am not comfortable with planes. They are incomprehensible. I try not to look up." He lifted his lips in a smirk and I smiled back.

"How old were you?"

"Five and twenty." When I must have looked shocked he added, "I'd lived through much by then."

I didn't care what he'd done in his twenty-five years, that was way too young to have it end, but I didn't argue. I took a sip of water. "But Innisfail? The veil? What exactly are they?"

Nibs, on her fifth packet of sugar, paused. "Where we come from." Nib's expression clearly screamed dislike. Again, this was information I could have used before now.

"The Brownie is correct. Innisfail is the land of the Fae." Aengus elaborated. "The veil was the door and originally Danu was the gatekeeper. It was his job to control who entered and exited Innisfail. That is until he disappeared and his consort, the Leannan Sidhe, took over and the more dangerous and vicious of the fae were allowed through. There was an uprising and the veil was closed completely."

I tried to digest it all. A special land of the fae. A gateway between realms. "Before you were buried alive, the fae could travel back and forth between their land and here? But now they can't, or couldn't until Excalibur was found?" He nodded. "The tomb was found a year ago, but there were fae here. They've been here my whole life. I'm cursed to see them, I should know."

Nibs crumpled up the empty sugar packet and threw it over her shoulder. "Didn't want to go." I guess that made sense. I've heard of people visiting a place and never wanting to leave, but I had a hard time believing the human realm was more interesting than a land of magic.

The look Aengus gave Nibs seemed kind. "Yes, some left

Innisfail because their life was better here, but for many, they had stayed too long in the human realm and were not allowed to return. They were considered tainted."

"Harsh." I could now kind of understand the Unseelie Queen's animosity.

Aengus absently picked up the crumpled paper ball and rolled it between his fingers. "You consider your ability to see the fae a curse?"

"Let's just say it's never helped me." Nibs let out a cry. "Aside from finding you," I added handing her another packet of sugar.

The server returned with our order. He smiled widely and encouraged us to enjoy our meal. The glamoured dimples didn't override the terrifyingly wide mouth and bulbous eyes beneath. Aengus thanked him and I tried to do the same without cringing.

I speared through the layer of cheese and bread on top of my soup, releasing a rush of delicious-smelling steam. As I dipped my spoon into the broth and blew on it, I noticed Aengus staring. I lifted my brow questioningly.

"I apologize, I was contemplating our different experiences. For you, a curse. For me, the only true family I had. Being *custos* saved my life." He lifted a piece of pineapple and set it in his mouth like it was a delicate flower. When he bit down his eyes closed and he hummed with so much pleasure, it made me almost blush.

"So, not a lot of pineapple where you're from?"

Aengus opened his eyes and looked away chagrined. "No. Not as such." Nibs stretched out her hand and Aengus handed her a large piece of cantaloupe. Nibs cooed over it, then took a massive bite, her cheeks ballooning around it.

"Is that why you were here?" I gestured to the casino. "The fruit?"

Aengus chuckled. "I requested someone meet me here. The fruit was just a lovely benefit."

"A Prince of Seelie?" He nodded. I thought of the Unseelie

queen, Saoirse, and the rest of the Unseelie fae. "Are the Seelie just as scary as the Unseelie?" I asked.

"No. And yes. All fae are dangerous and scary. The Seelie just hide it beneath beauty. It was a Seelie who turned me."

I was blowing on another spoonful of soup but set it back into the bowl. "Then why would you want to find one?"

"Because the Seelie also helped us close the veil the first time."

His gaze left me to a point over my shoulder. I followed his attention to the host leading another fae into our section of the diner. The fae's glamour only changed a few aspects. Aside from the pointed ears and dusky lavender skin, the fae looked like a well-muscled human male dressed in a dark, V-necked t-shirt and dark jeans.

Aengus tensed and his face hardened, only to quickly morph into a large smile when the fae called out to him. The smile didn't reach his eyes.

Aengus stood up, banging the table in his haste. I grabbed a hold of it to stop it from shaking. I watched as the fae flung his arms wide and crushed Aengus against him. I jolted at seeing Aengus flagrantly touch someone after what had just happened earlier. Since the fae didn't pass out, I had to assume his mojo didn't work on fae.

"Anguselus!" the fae exclaimed slapping Aengus's back. The name he used for Aengus sounded Latin. I liked the cadence of it. I slipped out of the booth and stepped closer. I learned a lot today, and if this fae knew Aengus, I wanted to hear more.

Aengus let go of the fae and took a step back. "I was not sure my words would reach you." There was a hesitancy to his tone.

"Where did you go, man? When the veil fell we searched for you. Until I got your message, I'd given up on finding you. Don't tell Mother I said that." The fae reached out and gripped Aengus's shoulder for a moment before letting it go.

The host snapped her menu and we all looked her way.

"Where would you like to sit, sir?" Her words polite, but her eyes were scolding.

"Come sit with us." Aengus pointed back toward our booth. The lavender fae waved away the host and her menu. She huffed loudly and stomped back to her podium. Then Aengus gestured to me. "Theo this is Imogen. Imogen this is, Theophilus — Theo." The way Aengus said his name made me take notice. It was weighted with familiarity, but also something I couldn't put my finger on. Theo was conventionally attractive in a human sense. Was this an old flame? Current one? An enemy?

"Honored to meet you, *Custos*." He placed a fist on his chest and bowed at the waist.

I just nodded my head. I didn't really know what dynamic I'd found myself in and it had me nervous and anxious.

"The *custos* still exist, then?" Aengus questioned him.

Theo shook his head. "Not in any capacity. The last fully trained *custos* died over a century ago. Over the years, it just became the term we use for a mixed human."

Even though this fae didn't seem to put as much derision in the words "mixed human" as the Unseelie Queen had, I still felt the censure. I had to admit, *Custos* sounded better.

We moved toward the table. Nibs was missing. Theo urged me with a shooing gesture to slide into the booth. I took a step back. No way was I going to sit penned in by a fae, handsome or not. Aengus noticed. He removed Excalibur, setting it on the table between the soup and the fruit, and then slid to the back of the booth. He pointed to the seat next to him. I smiled gratefully and sat down. Theo shrugged and took the bench across from us.

I felt Nibs latch onto my leg under the table. She scrambled up and disappeared into my hoodie pocket. Part of me wished I could join her.

"Your mother still leads the Seelie?" Aengus pressed himself against the wall to make sure he didn't touch me.

"Voted in again the last term. Imperator for life, just don't tell her I said that." Theo said, giving the soup a sniff. "You mind?" he asked, going for the spoon.

"Yes," Aengus answered and reached across the table to grab it. He set it down in front of me, having to move closer to do it. I turned toward him and our eyes locked. I gave a small smile. He smiled back, one side raising up higher than the other, and this time it reached his golden eyes. "Eat," he said softly. We stared for another moment until Aengus took a quick intake of breath and moved back closer to the wall. He turned away and looked at Theo as I bent forward to take a sip of my french onion. Theo scrutinized us both, but then raised his hand and called out for the server.

When the same college guy with bulbous eyes hustled to our table, Theo requested three stout beers and another french onion soup. Then he leaned on the table. "What happened? Where did you go?"

"I woke up when Excalibur was taken. I followed it to New York City." Aengus confirmed. "Finally, tracked it here."

Theo nodded. "Danu's still missing. There is no filter on what's coming through." He looked down at the sword and touched the blade hesitantly. He pulled his hand back, dark metal flakes coating his lavender fingertips. He rubbed them against his pants like they stung. "Is it supposed to look like that?"

"No," Aengus answered. "Excalibur is silent." He sounded worried.

I remembered the way the sword had felt at the museum. How the pop of energy had raced up my arm. Had it just been static electricity? I reached out to brush my fingers along the sword blade, again. Nothing happened, it just felt warm. My fingers came away clean.

"We need to close the veil before the Unseelie know we have the sword. That's all we need is another civil war," said Theo.

I listened as I ate my soup, feeling stronger with every sip. Focused on eating, it took me a moment to realize what the two men were talking about. I swallowed hard. The soup a solid lump in my throat. I coughed. "There might be an eensy wheensy problem with that," I wheezed. Aengus and Theo looked at me. I fought against the urge to hunch away from their gazes. "The Unseelie Queen already knows."

"How?" Aengus straightened. His body moving closer. I slid a few inches toward the end of the booth.

"Because I told her." Both men looked incredulous. I straightened and crossed my arms. "I didn't have a choice," I defended. "That's where I was earlier. This two-headed fae came and threatened Nibs if I didn't go with her. I met the queen, Saoirse, and she asked about the sword. I tried not to tell her, but there was this green knight, who could tell if I was lying. And she used magic—"

Aengus raised a hand to stop me from continuing and looked at Theo. "Is this Saoirse any different from the previous king?" Theo shrugged. "We need to figure out Excalibur and quickly."

Theo groaned. "I guess we need to speak with Mother."

Theo stood and Aengus urged me to stand as he slid out of the booth. He lifted Excalibur and slid the sword back into his belt. "Where are we going?" I asked.

Aengus shook his head. "Theo and I are going to go speak to the Leader of the Seelie. You are going to finish your soup and go home. I have put you in enough danger today as it is. If we do not meet again, Imogen, it has been a true pleasure."

Aengus put a fist to his chest and bowed. As he straightened, Theo placed a hand on his neck. It looked possessive. I didn't like it. As they both headed out of the diner I called out, "Wait!" Aengus paused and looked back. "So, you're just going to get buried alive again?"

"That is the plan." He gave his now familiar tight-lipped smirk.

"It's still a shitty plan," I repeated. He nodded and then continued with Theo out of the restaurant.

Chapter Twelve

The main door of the retirement home stood open to allow in the pleasant fall breeze when I arrived, my belly still warm with soup. Nibs had fallen asleep after all that sugar and hadn't stirred in my pocket the whole walk home. Through the shadowed screen door, I could just make out Everett sitting at the desk and a few residents watching *Law & Order*.

I stepped inside and nearly crashed into Ms. Carlton. No longer naked, or dressed in her usual nightgown, she wore a plaid sweater vest over a short-sleeved white button-up with tweed slacks. Her short, sparse, gray hair, usually wild and uncombed, was parted and slicked back. The sight wasn't a complete shock. Occasionally, Ms. Carlton regained her faculties, but during those episodes of clarity, she rarely spoke to me. She'd usually spent her limited time with my grandfather.

Today, it seemed she wanted me.

She made a shooing motion with her hand toward the hallway. "We've got things to talk about." Her tone was matter of fact. She must have seen the shock on my face. "I'm lucid, but it won't last so stop lollygagging."

At her insistence, I hustled through the kitchen to my bedroom, waving to everyone as I passed. Mr. Perez shuffled his way toward the back door with Milena, the nursing assistant on duty. "Enjoy your walk," I called, and he acknowledged me with a raised hand and a nod.

I opened the bedroom door and allowed Ms. Carlton to lead the way. She stopped only a few steps in, blocking my entrance. I looked over her shoulder to see why. A long, beautiful sword lay across my comforter. The sunlight through my window glinted across the blade, sending bursts of light to dance on the walls.

Ms. Carlton stepped closer and I followed. "Does that belong to you?" she asked.

"No, definitely not."

I pushed the door closed and moved around her to lean over the bed until my whole view was of the sword. The glassy smoothness of the blade called to me and I ran a hand along the metal, finding it not only warm and firm, but a slight tingle vibrated against my fingertips. Definitely real, and definitely in my bedroom. My first thought was Excalibur, which was crazy because the sword was pristine not corroded and crumbling apart. I couldn't even find a scratch. It looked as if the weapon had never been used.

"What have you got yourself into, Imogen?" she asked, her tone disapproving.

"I'm not sure what you mean, Ms. Carlton." I stood up straight, my back to the evidence, and scratched at my arm with nervous energy. Nibs shifted in my pocket and I hoped Ms. Carlton didn't notice. Mr. Friedman said the residents couldn't see fae like I could, not unless they had a *sul aos si*. He'd also said all the residents were part of a coven, but I'd unpack that later.

"Call me Jane, you've seen me naked after all," she said with a wink, but then her demeanor grew serious. "You brought a man into the house last night and it wasn't for fun."

She grabbed my desk chair, turned it around, and straddled it, lying her arms across the backrest. "I don't see you going out much, but I'm trusting you know what I mean by fun."

Should I be offended an eighty-five-year-old woman was commenting on my lack of sex life? I rested against the metal footboard and crossed my arms. "Yes, I know what you mean. And no, it wasn't for fun. He was hurt and I was helping."

"That's what Nibs said, too." Well, that answered whether she knew about the fae, or at least Nibbleink. I guess she really was putting out cookies for the Brownie. "It took us the whole morning to restore the wards he drained on the house. Is your friend coming back?" I shook my head no. "Good," she said with a quick nod. "The scuttlebutt around the ghosts says he's draining them dry of their magic. Some even seem to be gone completely."

"You know about ghosts?" Seriously, had I just walked through life oblivious to everything? Could everyone see ghosts and fae and I was just kept in the dark about it all? Because this was getting ridiculous.

"I'm a witch, of course I do. All witches can see the dead." That caught my attention. Witches could see ghosts? And Aengus said I could see fae because I had fae blood, but I also saw ghosts. What did that mean?

What was I?

I shifted and light from the sword blade bounced across my hand. I reached down and grabbed the hilt. A sizzle ran up my arm and exploded in my chest like a firework. Like the static pop that had happened in the museum when I'd touched the sword only more intense. I gasped. Could this be the same sword? That was impossible. And yet impossible seemed to be the M.O. of my last couple of days.

I clasped the hilt firmly and fought the urge to raise it above my head like a fantasy heroine. For one thing, the ceiling was too low, but for another, my luck the action would cause something terrible to happen. I sank down on the bed and laid the sword across my lap.

A sense of rightness filled me; as if the sword was mine, had always been mine, which again was impossible. Especially if it really was Excalibur.

"It's not supposed to be here." My voice was barely above a whisper.

Jane snorted. "With the amount of magic I can feel rolling off that sword, I believe it goes wherever it wants."

Maybe it had something to do with Aengus being here last night. Excalibur was integral to closing the veil and if this was *the* sword I needed to find him. The irony wasn't lost on me that I'd been furious that he'd stolen the sword in the first place and now I wanted to return it to him. My knuckles ached and I realized I had gripped the sword hilt harder at the thought of giving it away. Oh no, you don't, magic! Swords were cool, but I wasn't keeping it. Once I got rid of it, I could go back to the way things were — me ignoring the fae and them ignoring me. But I thought about what Jane said about how witches could see ghosts. "Jane, can I ask you something?"

She swirled one arm in a "keep it moving" gesture. "The sanity clock is ticking. You got something to ask, make it quick."

"I'm just wondering if a person can be both a witch and be part fae?" I knew my mom and Grandpa had fae blood. Grandpa definitely knew about the fae and Mom was his daughter. I didn't know if they were witches too, but if they weren't that would mean Geoffrey Corben, my newly realized father, was.

Jane nodded. "It's rare, but it happens. They also don't tend to live long. It's one of the reasons your grandfather set up this house." Her no-nonsense expression softened.

"What do you mean, don't tend to live long?" My words came out more shrill than I'd intended. Nibs shifted again in my hoodie pocket but this time popped her head out the side. She looked at me then at Jane. She grinned and made her way down my leg and then up the old woman's tweed one. Nibs settled herself cross legged on Jane's lap adjusting her tartan sarong so it would lie straight. Jane took a finger and lightly scratched Nibs behind her ears. The Brownie closed her eyes in pure happiness. The little traitor. Nibs had threatened to bite my finger off when I'd tried that.

"There are two reasons the Cailleach Fae die young. One," Jane lifted her index finger, "fae magic makes witch magic unruly and chaotic. Death by spell is how many go. But two," she lifted her middle finger, "there are fae who desire to possess the chaotic power and they have ways to acquire it. Ways that don't allow the Cailleach Fae to live." She dropped her hand over the chair back.

I could see ghosts, yes, and the fae, but I wasn't this Calliyock Jane was talking about. I couldn't be. "I don't have magic. After twenty plus years, I think I would have noticed."

Jane set Nibs on the ground before standing up and pacing a few steps to the door and back. She sighed heavily and rubbed the back of her neck. "You have magic. Your grandfather never forgave your mother for hooking up with a witch."

"You knew my father Geoffrey Corben?"

"No, he was long gone before we got here. Later, after your mother skipped town, your grandfather did everything in his power to make sure you were safe. Including," Jane paused and looked away. I worried she'd slipped back into her dementia fog, but when she turned toward me her eyes were hard and clear. "Including hiring Mary and I to lock away your magic."

Lock away my magic?

"It's weird, Mary should be here to tell you about this, too," Jane murmured, dropping her arms to her sides. "Where did she go?" She moved her head as if searching for her partner.

"Mary's been dead for two years. Remember?" I asked gently.

Jane rubbed her temple. "Oh yes, you're right. I forget sometimes." Jane's words were suddenly sounding weaker and I knew we'd only have a few minutes more. Not nearly long enough to answer all my questions.

"If you and Mary sealed away my magic, does that mean it's gone forever?"

Jane shook her head. "I wish it was. It'll only put you in danger."

I opened my mouth to ask more questions when a shriek reached through the walls from outside. I jumped to my feet and both Jane and I rushed toward the door. I swiped my cell from the dresser, not wanting to be caught without it like earlier. "Stay inside!" I yelled to Nibs over my shoulder.

We ran into the kitchen and straight out the back door. The late afternoon sun had begun its descent toward the top of the mountains to the west. Beneath the large, fifty-year-old elm, Milena was screaming for help and waving her arms above her head. Mr. Perez was nowhere in sight.

Barely landing on any of the steps, I launched myself into the yard and ran toward her. My right hand felt heavy. I glanced down and saw I still held the sword. I quickly dropped the tip as I ran, not wanting to accidentally run the poor CNA through. As I reached her, she pointed frantically upward.

The tree creaked above us as we all looked. Mr. Perez lay across a large, lower branch, clinging to it with both arms and legs. His eyes were full of terror and his dark skin looked pale. How did he get up there?

I glanced over my shoulder and saw Jane was still on the porch. "Get Everett." Her nod was delayed and her steps were hesitant as she turned to go inside. I hoped she was still lucid enough to do as I asked.

Branches creaked again and my gaze returned to the foliage. I worried Mr. Perez had lost his grip, but he still clung tight. "Did you climb up there?" I asked gently.

His scathing look was answer enough, but he still said, "No."

I remembered all the residents were apparently part of a coven. Witches. "Just curious, umm, could you, like, use your magic to get down?"

"My magic, is no what it was, *es débil.*"

I raised the hand not holding the sword as if to give him a

comfort pat, even though he was at least ten feet up. "Okay. Just hold on. We'll get you down."

"*Ay gracias, eres un tesoro.*" The leaves above him rattled, and he twisted so he could look above. "There is something ungodly up here. *Rapido, por favor.*"

Out of the corner of my eye, I saw Milena slowly backing away. Her tall messy bun bouncing from one side of her head to the other. Her eyes focused on the tree branches. I thought about telling her to run inside and make sure Jane had found Everett, when something large descended toward us. The sound of snapping branches echoed around the yard. The mass falling from above slammed to the ground with a solid thump. I jumped back. The nurse wasn't as quick. She fell to the ground, holding her face as blood seeped through her fingers. "*¿Estás bien?*" Mr. Perez called down. I looked at the nurse and she nodded with glassy eyes.

"We're okay," I called as I moved toward the mass of fur. My sword held out in front as if I knew how to use it.

It took a minute to register what lay on the ground until I saw her head, folded nearly beneath her body. A doe. Her entire chest cavity had been ripped open, white ribs pulled out and away, and all the organs removed. Eaten? Just like the horses Diana had shown me in the news. Just like the mule deer buck in the desert.

I needed to get Mr. Perez down now! If what had killed all those animals was what had pulled him into the tree, he was in more danger than just falling. My grip on the sword clenched and unclenched as my brain raced through different possibilities.

Milena stood on shaky legs, one hand still on her face, blood welling between her fingers and staining her scrubs. One of the deer's hooves must have sliced her cheek as it fell. "Go inside. Make sure Everett comes out right now." Her bottom lip trembled, but she nodded and ran toward the house, her gait uneven and stumbling.

Scanning the branches above Mr. Perez I finally saw it, whatever it was. A pale grey shadow slithered along a very thick branch, its body nearly the same diameter. I yelped and jerked back when its long leathery tail dropped and curled completely around a branch directly overhead, squeezing hard enough to make the wood protest.

"A scolex," Nibs said by my feet. In surprise, I looked down at the Brownie. She had changed from her makeshift sarong and was now wearing the 80s Rocker Barbie outfit, the gold lamé jumpsuit glinting in the setting sun. I wanted to reprimand her for not listening and staying inside, but I also needed to know what we were up against, and Nibs had the knowledge.

"This thing killed the mule deer, right?" I asked and Nibs nodded. "How did it get here?" Both incidents had been well out of the city.

"Followed your blood." Nibs stared up into the tree, black eyes unblinking.

"What?" Then, I remembered my sliced palm. And the drops of blood on the desert sand. Great. I'd lured a dangerous carnivorous fae worm straight into town and into my backyard. Was the deer the only thing it had eaten along the way?

The back door slammed against the side of the house as it flew open. Everett was by my side in moments. He immediately noticed the deer and mouthed the question "Bear?" I shrugged unable to give a real answer. Everett gazed into the tree to find Mr. Perez. "Don't worry we'll get you down," he assured. Then he turned to me, looking like he was going to say something, but then paused. His expression was confused. "Is that a sword?" He pointed to my hand.

I nodded. "It's a long story." I raised the sword to gesture toward Mr. Perez. "Do you think you could catch him?" Everett looked unsure, possibly of the whole situation. I smiled. "Remember all those times, you thought something was weird and I explained it away?"

"Mm-hmm." He looked at me expectantly.

"Well, something weird *is* going on and I'm not going to explain it away. I promise I'll tell you everything, but right now I need you to help Mr. Perez. He's in real danger."

Everett squinted at me in frustration but stepped directly under Mr. Perez. He reached out his arms, his massive biceps stretching the fabric of his scrubs. "The van wasn't attacked by a bear, was it?" he asked over his shoulder.

"Not exactly."

"Didn't think so," he mumbled, then spoke loudly and firmly. "Mr. Perez, I'm going to need you to roll to the side and fall. I'll catch you."

"Watch out!" Nibs squawked.

At the Brownie's voice, Everett leaped backwards, his eyes wide. Nibs had obviously dropped her glamour. "Later, I promise," I cried and urged Everett to get to Mr. Perez. Above us, the gigantic corpse-colored snake dropped its head from out of the yellowed leaves. Its head was much longer and wider than a snake's with an underbite holding two massive canines that matched up with the two above it. They didn't look like snake fangs, but more like the teeth of a mammal carnivore. And its eyes weren't reptile eyes either, more like a goat's.

The scolex now hung low by its wrapped tail. With a twist it swung toward us, mouth open and threatening. A forked tongue flicked out and back in. The size reminded me of the exhibit of the Titanoboa that had visited the museum a few years back, the inconceivable size setting off every primordial prey instinct in my body. At least Everett was unable to see the beast, or I doubt I could have gotten him to stay beneath the tree. He continued to encourage Mr. Perez to fall, waving his arms like a windmill. The older man clutched the branch tighter and shook his head.

The sword in my hand warmed again. I gazed down at it. If it was Excalibur, it was a priceless artifact. Magic or not it should be in a museum. I couldn't use it. Could I? The snake fae dipped toward an unsuspecting Everett, mouth open. Gods of antiquities forgive me, priceless or not, I couldn't let the scolex eat anyone. Two hands on the hilt, I swung toward its head.

And completely missed.

The momentum nearly spun me in a circle. I dropped the sword tip into the ground to stop myself. But my swing drew the scolex's attention. It twisted to lunge back toward me and I braced to attack again. This time the sword connected with the scales, biting in. The fae bellowed and jerked away, tearing the sword from my grip. In that moment, Mr. Perez got up the courage and toppled from the tree branch. Everett caught him, letting out a big huff of air, but he didn't drop him. "Go!" I urged, waving my arm toward the house.

Still hanging from the branches, the scolex writhed, the sword stuck tight. The hilt swung wildly opposite each time the snake fae moved. I had to keep ducking, trying not to be hit by fae or sword.

Behind me, the clink of a large metal object thunked to the ground between the house and the tree. I half turned, trying to keep my eye on the fae. Across the yard, Mr. Friedman stood on the porch with his arms outstretched over his walker. One of his antiques, a revolutionary war musket, lay in the grass. "I saw the dead deer from the window," he said by way of explanation. "Kick its fae ass!"

Oh my god, didn't anyone have a weapon that wasn't supposed to be in a museum?!

I ran to pick up the musket, holding it like a club.

Hesitantly, I took a few steps closer. The snake fae coiled, its body pulling together to strike, sword sticking out like an arm. This was insanity. Mr. Perez was safe. I didn't have fighting skills. The art of fleeing sat comfortably in my wheelhouse. I needed to run away, but I didn't. How many more innocent beings would die if this creature wasn't stopped? With a primal yell that definitely telegraphed my movements, I swung.

The snake fae tried to pull back, but I still caught it on the nose.

It screeched loudly and spun away. I dived to the ground as the attached sword nearly took off my head. When I straightened, I raised my rifle club and swung again while it was still distracted. The musket connected with its neck and this time the snake fae's movements unseated the sword. With a bounce, it fell free. I dropped the musket and dove for it.

The scolex dove, too, and dropped lower as it tried to grab me.

Heart pounding, I rolled and came up with the sword in my hand, hero style. If I wasn't focused on not dying, I'd be pretty proud of myself.

When the scolex twisted again to strike at me, I gripped the hilt as hard as I could and brought it down right where its head met its body. The sword didn't get stuck this time. Instead, it cut cleanly through the leathery hide as if the blade had been sharpened to a razor's edge. The head thumped to the ground and above in the branches I heard the whole snake body crashing through the foliage to follow.

I snatched Nibs up from the ground and dashed away as the body hit hard enough to make the ground shake. Leaves floated down around us like yellow cherry blossoms.

"Imogen!" Startled, I looked over to see Aengus running toward me from the open back gate, his long coat whipping around behind him like a cape and his chest still bare. He stopped and stared at the pile of snake fae. Its color was more appropriate now that it was actually a corpse.

"I killed the scolex." I said my voice quiet and unbelieving. "With a sword."

Aengus pointed at the snake fae, "That is not a scolex." Then he pointed at the sword in my hand. "And why do you have my sword?"

"What do you mean it's not a scolex?"

The snake fae twitched.

I looked down at Nibs. "I thought you said it was a scolex?"

She shrugged. "Guess not."

The pale, leathery skin seemed to tremble. One of the coils definitely shifted. "If it isn't a scolex, what is it?" I asked. When Aengus didn't answer right away, I glanced over at him. He was staring at the sword.

"She is whole," he said softly. "How is it possible?"

"What do you mean? I found this sword on my bed." Swords did not magically appear in bedrooms.

Aengus lifted his coat away to show his empty belt. "I felt her disappear."

"That's impossible." I glanced from the empty belt to the sword in my hand in disbelief.

"She goes where she will. Here was the first place I looked."

I blinked. "Here? Why?"

"Well, clearly I thought you may be in danger. The Unseelie could have returned. Or whomever stole the sword might have... well, they could have... I did spend the night here. They might have tracked me here." He rubbed the back of his neck and gave a crooked smile. "It seemed logical to check on you."

Aengus ran here to check on me? And counter to his explanation, it was in no way logical. Which meant he came here for an illogical reason. How did I even feel about that? What I felt was nothing, because he was a 1,400-year-old vampire who can't be touched and planned to be buried alive, again. Now that's what I call logic! Too bad it didn't halt the flip of my insides as I gazed at him. Flustered, I pointed to his bare chest, "Don't you own another shirt?"

Aengus jolted at my words and looked down at himself, then back up at me. "Actually, no." Maybe Everett had an extra scrub top hanging around. I nearly snorted as a laugh tried to bubble out. As if that would make him less hot.

Aengus motioned toward the sword. "May I have her?"

I looked down at the sword. "Then it really is Excalibur?" I ran a hand over the flat of the blade. The sunlight raced over the metal like a droplet of liquid star. "I thought it was. It felt like it was, but I wasn't sure."

"Yes, she is unmistakable." He reached for Excalibur. I hesitated. For some reason I didn't want to let her go, but that was ridiculous. Aengus needed the sword. The snake fae lying not quite dead on my lawn had entered my world through a doorway. If Aengus didn't close that doorway, more than just the wildlife was going to suffer. Probably already had suffered. And if the snake fae really wasn't dead Aengus was better equipped to tackle it. I reached out with the hilt first for Aengus to grab. He smiled wistfully. I let go as his fingers twisted around the handle.

And the sword dropped to the ground nearly taking Aengus with it.

He looked at me, then down at the sword in shock. He reached and wrapped both hands around the hilt. With effort he lifted it, acting as if the Excalibur weighed as much as a clunky cast iron skillet and not a well-balanced weapon. "That is odd," he mumbled. I silently agreed. The sword had been surprisingly light when I'd held it. And this was the same person who had ripped a fence post from the ground one-handed. Whatever the fae had done to him, he was certainly stronger than a regular person. A sword should be nothing in comparison.

Nibs giggled at him, then dashed closer to the sprawled snake fae. "Be careful," I scolded, but the Brownie just waved her hand at me, as if to sweep away my concern. In the distance a siren blared, growing closer each revolution. No doubt, Everett had called emergency services. I hoped Mr. Perez and Milena were okay.

Aengus was taking test swings with the sword. His face pinched in irritation. Or confusion. While he ran through interconnected moves, I asked him about the Seelie court. He answered distractedly. "I did not reach the court. I left Theo at the door to search for Excalibur. Why is she so heavy?" he mused, moving the sword from one hand to the other.

"Genny?" Nibs squeaked and I could hear the fear. Both

Aengus and I turned toward her. The snake fae was definitely moving now. All the coils were twisting and curling in on themselves.

"Nibs get away!" I demanded and the Brownie ran through the grass back to my side. "What is it?" I demanded of Aengus again.

"Hydra," he answered. "Young ones only have a single head."

The writhing body rolled, bringing the severed, headless neck into full view. A pearlescent film had grown over the open stump and like a pulsing heartbeat, two lumps pushed against it. Two heads growing where one had been.

"How do we kill it?" I thought about how much damage it had done with only one head. What would happen when it had more?

"Nearly impossible, even if we were in Innisfail. Danu tried never to let them through the veil."

"Couldn't we find this missing Danu?"

Nibs scampered up my leg. "Not missing. Dead," she said with intense anger.

Aengus smiled, but it was a sad smile. "We do not know if he is dead."

Nibs rolled her eyes. "Gone over a thousand years? Dead! Murdered!"

Aengus opened his mouth to respond, which I knew from experience wouldn't change Nibs' mind, so I stepped in. "We need to get the hydra out of here before it causes more harm. If we can't kill it, is there a way to get it back to Innisfail?"

"Possibly, but we need to speak with the Seelie Court."

For a moment, I was five again, staring at my grandpa in the rearview mirror, promising to stay away from the fae. Promising to stay safe. I could practically hear those promises shattering around me. The pieces scattered on the ground, too small to be worth anything. If I walked away now, would I be able to salvage my old normal life? I looked at the incapacitated — and decapitated — hydra at my feet and severely doubted it.

Wood creaked and snapped to our left and part of the fence surrounding the backyard crashed to the ground. The Green Knight from the Unseelie Court stomped through, axe raised high.

Normal life? What normal life?

Chapter Thirteen

Nibs squeaked and clawed her way into my hoodie pocket. Aengus took a step in front of me and raised Excalibur. His arms trembled with the effort. Without thinking, I rushed to the dropped musket, grabbing it up as the Green Knight entered and paused just past the destroyed fence.

If it was possible, they looked even larger out in the open. The vines and leaves seemed to pulse with life beneath the light of the setting sun. The Unseelie queen had sent them after Aengus and the sword, but how had it known to come here? Maybe they had a way to track the sword. Either that or I was now attracting fae to my doorstep, just as I had the hydra.

Near the tree, the hydra roiled and caught the attention of the Green Knight. One large step had them nearly on top of the snake fae. They brought down the axe and chopped the hydra like a chef chopping a carrot. The pieces turned black and crumpled in on themselves like ash.

The knight turned their gaze back toward us, axe blade held out before them, dripping black ooze.

"Give me Excalibur," the Green Knight demanded with a voice like rustling leaves.

Aengus lowered Excalibur to his side and he reached out a hand in greeting. "Gawain, my old friend, it has been ages." I recognized that name. Another of King Arthur's men. Nothing could surprise me now. Maybe Robin Hood would show up next.

The Green Knight didn't move. "Gawain is dead. I am another. Relinquish Excalibur." Their words were brisk and Aengus reacted as if he was slapped.

"Rest in peace, my friend." Aengus whispered, his face stricken.

The Green Knight gestured with their axe. "The sword or your death."

"Whoever you are, I have one duty, one purpose, and you will not take it from me." Aengus widened his stance and raised Excalibur, the weight of the sword still affecting his movements. I gripped the musket by the barrel and rested the stock on my shoulder. The weight gave a false assurance. My eyeline lingered on the pile of black, crumbled hydra and knew I was no match for whatever came next.

"You need to go inside, Imogen." Aengus gave me a quick glance, then turned back to the knight as he spoke, eyeing him with resolve.

"What about you?" My modern sensibilities chafed under the chivalry despite having considered the same thing just moments earlier.

"If I enter the house, I will drain the wards of their power again and I do not think your coven has enough strength to repair them twice."

"You're correct, so keep your distance," Jane's voice called from behind us. I turned to look and felt Nibs scramble out of the hoodie pocket. She climbed to my free shoulder and stood, waving. Jane and the residents had lined up across the back porch, Mr. Perez noticeably missing. I'd been certain Jane had fallen back into dementia, but her eyes looked clear and steely. Where had she been when I was fighting the hydra? Having a witch in my corner might have been nice.

The Green Knight stepped closer, drawing all of our attention. "Your choice is made."

Aengus adjusted his grip on the hilt. "Imogen, you should go now." The knight's axe came down and Aengus lifted the sword to defend, the effort plainly visible on his face. The weapons collided the sound sharp and loud. Aengus deflected the blow, but he stumbled as the sword seemed to pull him down. His knee hit the ground.

"Vampire! The Green Knight is impossible to stop in its current form," Jane yelled.

"Witch," Aengus snapped back as he regained his feet. "I am well aware." He moved to circle the knight, not quite running away, but staying firmly out of reach as the knight swung again. Nibs still on my shoulder, I gripped my musket tighter and tried to stay out of the way. I was no swordsmith. What kind of help could I possibly be, maybe I should head to the house.

"Shut up and listen," Jane growled at him. "We can part the vines that encase the form beneath. It's the only way to stop it, but you'll only get one shot. We won't be able to cast the spell twice."

Aengus dropped the sword's tip so it touched the ground, letting the weight rest for a moment. "Understood," he answered, then with a heave lifted the sword once more and stepped into the knight's reach.

The coven on the porch started to chant. Their monotone and indecipherable words rose and fell like a working machine. My attention divided between Aengus and the witches, I didn't realize Nibs was trying to get my attention until she yanked hard on my earlobe.

"Ow! What the hell, Nibs." I nearly swatted her from my shoulder in surprise.

"Stop them," she said pointing to Jane and the rest.

"Nibs, the knight will kill Aengus. Then it'll kill us. We can't stop." To punctuate my words the axe came down and nearly took off Aengus's arm at the elbow. He turned barely in time, so that the axe only ripped through the jacket, exposing his arm.

"No," Nibs said her voice rising in panic. "They can't. They mustn't."

The chanting rose in a crescendo. Beneath the voices I could hear the slither and rustle of moving leaves. The Green Knight halted mid swing, the axe head dropping to the ground, biting into the dirt. The vines that wove around the head like a helmet unraveled, like snakes escaping a den, until an entire face and neck were visible.

The face beneath was male, bearded with blonde hair turning to gray at the chin. He had a strong widow's peak and a long straight nose. The Green Knight, now with the head of a human man, looked out at Aengus and then his gaze fell on me. His eyes widened. He fell to one knee.

The coven continued to chant.

Aengus grunted with great effort and swung toward the knight's now uncovered head.

Next to my ear, Nibs let out a guttural squeak and leaped for Aengus's arm as he swung. She barely made the jump clinging to the fabric of his coat, before pulling herself up to race down his arm and bite his hand, holding on like a dog gripping a chew toy.

"Nibs!" I screeched, reaching toward her even though she was too far away for me to grab.

Aengus bellowed and released the sword to fling her off him, which, now too heavy for Aengus to hold in one hand, fell ungracefully to the ground with a thump. Followed by Nibs' tiny body hitting the ground hard and bouncing up against the Green Knight's axe before laying still.

"No, no, no, no, no, no, no," I heard the word in my ears, before realizing I was repeating them myself. I rushed to Nibs, despite how close she lay to the Green Knight, and dropped to my knees.

Behind me, Aengus snapped, "Has she gone mad?" I ignored him, but I didn't argue. I had no idea why Nibs had reacted the way she had. I gently picked up the Brownie, her arms and legs limp and swaying. She felt fragile, a marionette held together with strings as I held her against my shoulder. Only her chest rising and falling lightly beneath my hand assured me that she lived.

"Imogen, you need to step back," Aengus urged. Over my shoulder, I watched him struggle to lift Excalibur for another swing.

Clutching Nibs, I rose and stepped out of the Green Knight's shadow. I peered up at the face, a foot above me even though he was kneeling. His human head sat diminutively within the mass of greenery. I could almost see where the spell was holding back the vines and leaves, a shimmer that ringed his neck like an Elizabethan collar.

His brow furrowed over his glassy eyes, holding back tears. "You're already grown. I've missed it all."

"I don't understand," I whispered taking another step back.

Suddenly he looked around, searching, "Is Mira, here? Did she ever forgive me?"

My mother? How did he know my mother? Bits of information became puzzle pieces falling into place. The Green Knight had been at the Unseelie Court. Dennriall said he owed my father. And Nibs had been sent by my father. Nibs' reaction when Aengus had tried to attack the knight.

"Move, now!" Aengus demanded.

I stayed still, shaking my head. "I can't. I think he's my father."

The Green Knight closed his eyes and nodded.

Aengus jerked mid swing, causing the sword to dip until Excalibur's point sunk deep into the ground. The chanting from the porch continued. He turned his gaze to me. "Your father?"

I nodded.

The term father was hard to process. It was like a foreign word that sounded familiar, but I couldn't quite understand it. In the abstract, I knew I had to have a father, but in reality, he had never truly existed. But he had a name. Geoffrey Corben. And now he had a face.

I rubbed Nibs gently with my thumb. Why hadn't she woken yet? I looked at my father. "Nibs said you sent her?"

Geoffrey's entire face transformed when he chortled with amusement. "She is a singular being. I less sent her as pointed her in your direction." Then his expression saddened. "She saved my life, but I'm helpless to save hers. She has touched my axe. Death is only a matter of time."

I fought the urge to clutch Nibs tighter. I barely got out a strangled, "What?"

Aengus sighed. "There are only a few things that can destroy the fae. That axe is one of them. You saw what it did to the hydra."

I couldn't seem to take a full breath. "But there has to be a way to save her." A vision of Nibs crumbling into ashes made my heart stutter.

My father's gaze dropped to Nibs. "I've come to understand that for the fae nothing is impossible." He reached out as if to touch the Brownie, but realized his hand was too large and pulled it back. "I told her stories of my daughter... you... while I was trapped. I think that is why she asked to find you for me. I wished I had more stories, but you were only four when I left."

Daughter. Hearing the word said by the virtual stranger before me was both exhilarating and confusing. The man was my father, but I didn't know him at all. There definitely wasn't a Hallmark card for this situation.

"You left when I was four?" I scrutinized him, but nothing about him was familiar. "I don't remember you."

Geoffrey searched the yard again. "Mira, your mother, she should have explained what happened."

That was the second time he'd mentioned my mother as if she should be with me. "I haven't seen my mother since I was five," I told him. "And I don't really remember her either. Why is that? Why don't I remember you both?"

Geoffrey immediately glared at the chanting witches behind me. "Stolen memories."

I turned to look at the witches as well. Had they really stolen my memories? I thought about how my grandfather had kept me in the dark about everything else and I had to concede taking my memories seemed like something he'd have done to keep me safe. It was becoming harder and harder not to be really angry with him. Best intentions or not.

"Why did you both leave?" I asked, my voice sounding young and childlike.

Geoffrey smiled sadly and opened his mouth maybe to answer, but at that moment all three of us seemed to register the absence of the chanting at the same time and looked toward the porch. The witches had stopped. The residents leaned on each other. Clearly exhausted. I turned to my father and saw the shimmering collar had dissipated, the vines already starting to slither upwards.

"We can't cast the spell again," Mr. Friedman called to us.

The Green Knight stood. I could barely make out my father's features beneath the growing foliage. "Run!" he roared.

Chapter Fourteen

"Don't follow, Imogen . He's only after the sword," Aengus called to me as we raced out of the backyard. He almost waddled as he tried to hold the sword in both hands and still run. The blade nearly dragged against the ground. He looked like a toddler carrying a heavy weight. I'd laugh if we weren't being chased by a giant plant man with an axe who also happened to be my dad.

I knew Aengus was right. He had the sword — the only thing the Green Knight wanted. Aengus would go to the Seelie and close the veil. My part in all this was done. But it wasn't like I could forget that my father was alive and currently a walking topiary. And what about Nibs?

I cradled my hoodie pocket as we ran, Nibs' unconscious, tiny body curled inside. I hadn't realized how isolated I'd felt until Nibs showed up. Suddenly there was someone I could be completely honest with every weird aspect of my life. It wasn't always easy. Nibs could be infuriatingly difficult, but that was what family was like, right? I couldn't accept she would die. My father had said nothing was impossible with the fae and I needed to believe that. The Seelie had to help her. I'd make them. Somehow.

A flash of guilt raced through my gut and I knew it was Grandpa's edict demanding I stay away from the fae. Sorry Grandpa. I tried to follow your lead, I really did. I looked down at Nibs in my pocket then over at Aengus. "I have to follow, I don't have a choice."

Orange, fiery clouds streaked across the sky as the sun journeyed behind the mountains. Shadows stretched their fingers over the houses and lawns as we made our way through the quiet neighborhood. Very few people saw me running like a madwoman, and only a man walking his dog called out to ask if I was alright. I gave him a wave and a wide smile, which seemed to scare him away. Luckily, no one would see Aengus with his glamour, which meant the long sword was hidden, too.

We paused to let two cars drive past so we could cross the street. Beside me, I heard metal ring out like a gong. "*Moecha putida*," Aengus swore loudly.

I looked over. Excalibur lay on the cement, Aengus bent over it. Even in the low light, I could see the strain on his face as he yanked on the sword hilt. It didn't move.

"Are you swearing in Latin?" I moved to his side.

"Habit." He tried to lift the sword, again. In a huff, he jumped back. "Damn the gods! I cannot raise her." With an open palm he gestured toward the sword. "You will need to take her. She has refused me."

"What? That can't be right." I looked down at the sword in confusion.

"Grab the sword. We need to make haste."

Disbelieving, I bent down and gripped the hilt. Warmth coursed up my arm and through my body, wrapping itself like a security blanket. I easily lifted Excalibur. Even though I'd held it earlier, and had even taken the head off the hydra, knowing the sword really was *the* Excalibur made it different. Something I'd thought pure fiction was real in my grip. I shivered with excitement. "I'm holding King Arthur's sword," I said in wonderment.

"She was never Arthur's sword. Let us away." Without explaining, Aengus started to run.

I followed, one hand holding the sword, the other still keeping Nibs safe in my pocket. "You need to stop doing that!"

Aengus, freed from the drag of Excalibur, had started to pull ahead of me. He looked over his shoulder. "Doing what?"

"Saying Excalibur wasn't Arthur's sword. Or that you're Lancelot, but you're not Lancelot. You're breaking my reality."

Aengus slowed so he was running alongside me. "But it is truth."

I groaned. "Never mind."

We continued to run, heading towards Carson Street and presumably the Seelie Court. Now that I held the sword, there was also no way to hide it from view. I grabbed the hilt, letting the blade rest against my forearm behind me, and ran. I really hoped if anyone saw me they'd just think I was LARPing.

In the distance, I could hear a steady thumping that could only be the Green Knight. Each footfall sounded like a massive tree trunk hitting the ground. Whatever head start my father had managed to give us was rapidly dwindling.

I was glad that the residents were likely safe and able to retreat into the house behind the wards. We'd discuss my missing memories when I returned. I ignored the implied "if I returned" that my brain threw in.

Aengus took the lead, heading in the direction of the capitol building.

Even in the fall, Curry Street had a good number of tourists. Aengus's glamour caused most to move instinctually out of our way, but some didn't. Pushing through people without showing off the really large sword in my hand was nearly impossible. When anyone caught sight of Excalibur, I just yelled, "It's a prop. I'm with the theater." No one noticed the eight-foot-tall tree-man brandishing an axe thundering down the road alongside the sidewalk. I wished I couldn't either.

The corner of West 4th Street curved before us. The concussive sound of the Green Knight's stride echoed off the surrounding buildings, causing severe disorientation. If I didn't have Aengus to focus on I would no doubt have stopped, unable to continue.

I glanced over my shoulder and a scream threatened to explode from me. The Green Knight seemed close enough I could have reached out and touched him. My fear snatched all my momentum and I froze. The Green Knight raised his axe to swing. Aengus yanked hard on my arm and half dragged me toward the cross street. The axe slammed on the asphalt, hard enough to spark, but the Green Knight didn't move to follow us. I noted that where the axe landed wouldn't have hit me even if Aengus hadn't yanked me away. Maybe my father was more aware than we thought.

I fell against a parked car, thankful it didn't have an alarm, and took deep heaving breaths. Aengus stopped, too, but he didn't even look winded, not a drop of sweat on his forehead. We stared at the Green Knight standing sentry on the corner. "He cannot enter the Seelie Court without permission," Aengus explained.

"Good," I wheezed, catching my breath. I reached inside my hoodie pocket to make sure Nibs still breathed and sighed with relief when her little chest moved.

When I finally could breathe again, we stepped into a recessed doorway of a three-story office building. Aengus pulled on the handle, but it banged against the lock. He pulled on it again, a little harder. The glass in the door rattled. I reached over his arms and pushed the doorbell button on the wall.

Sheepishly, Aengus let go.

A few moments later, a strikingly beautiful woman opened it, forcing us to move as the door swung outward. She wore a glamour, and like Theo, it was barely needed to alter her features. A slight rounding of the ears, shrinking the large luminous eyes, and lessening some of the sharper alien features. Honestly, she looked like a runway model either way. "May I help you?" Her words were polite, her expression said otherwise.

"We are here to see Lady Aurnia." Aengus answered.

"You'll have to make an appointment." The woman tried to shut the door.

Aengus placed his foot between the door and the jamb. "We are here at the request of Theophilus."

The woman looked skeptical.

I lifted Excalibur. "We have this."

She stepped to the side and gestured for us to enter. The lobby inside was ultra-modern with different shades of gray and white and chairs that didn't look the least bit comfortable. Considering the less-than-friendly greeting, it might actually have been on purpose. The only color was one lone teal pillow and an abstract painting on the wall. "Wait here," she said pointing to the uncomfortable chairs before she disappeared down a light gray hallway.

"This is the Seelie Court?" I whispered to Aengus. He sat down stiffly on one of the chairs. His hands were balled into fists, and they pressed against his thighs until the leather of the gloves squeaked.

"The latest one." He nodded his head, but otherwise seemed to remain unmoving.

"Where was it before?"

He didn't straighten but looked askance at me. "The original courts are still in Innisfail, but in my time, the new courts were near the first break in the veil, over the island of Eire. I believe it is called Ireland in this age. More doorways opened following the first."

"Why even come here to begin with? Especially, if they weren't allowed to return." I could almost understand the human desire to enter a land of magic, but what would draw the fae to such a mundane place?

I slumped against the back of the stiff chair and let the tip of

Excalibur rest on the fake wood flooring, as the adrenaline started to fade and leave weakness in its wake. My legs trembled and nausea rolled over me like a wave. The bit of soup this afternoon had not been enough. Not with all the fighting and running and nearly dying. My eyesight dimmed at the edges. I clocked the futuristic-looking trash can. Just in case.

Aengus clenched and unclenched his fist and he seemed to visibly force his shoulders away from his ears. I didn't think he'd answer, but then he cracked his neck and looked at me. "I am unaware of when the veil opened for the first time, but I know by my time, there were many unable to return. The lure of humanity had been too much. Humans are constantly creating and altering their lives. Time moves differently in faerie. Each time the fae visit there is something new to enjoy. Watching the lives of humans became a drug and some ultimately lost their home realm to the addiction."

"So, humans were a Netflix show the fae couldn't resist binging?"

Aengus paused and I imagined he was combing through the information he'd consumed while he slept in the tomb. Finally, he nodded. "It would appear so."

Surreptitiously, I peeked at Nibs in my hoodie. She was still unconscious but had rolled herself into a tight ball. I didn't know if it was a good sign that she curled up. Didn't bugs curl up just before the end? I locked that mode of thinking down tight. Nibs was not dying today. I cupped my hand protectively around the outside of the pocket. There had to be a way to help her. I wouldn't accept any other outcome.

We sat in silence as total dark fell outside and the windows surrounding us turned into mirrors. Finally, the fae who'd let us in returned and ordered us to follow her.

Standing was harder than I thought it would be, especially as I tried not to jostle Nibs. My legs felt barely attached to my body and my first attempt failed. When I moved to try again, I found Aengus's gloved hands in my face.

"Let me help," he said quietly.

I carefully gripped his hand. The warm soft leather felt comforting against my palm. I rose as slow as possible to keep the darkness threatening at the edge of my vision from overwhelming me. I didn't pass out, but I listed to the side for a moment before straightening. I noticed Aengus had held out his other arm to catch me. It must have been instinctual, because if I'd fallen into him, touching his bare chest again might have made me a Sleeping Beauty with no prince to kiss me awake.

At the thought of a kiss I noticed we were now standing very close. Lean muscle peeking through the open coat. I fought the urge to reach past the fabric and run a hand down his chest. Luckily, my only free hand was filled with a sword hilt.

Aengus narrowed his eyes and his brow furrowed. I felt him squeeze my fingers. Was he concerned? He'd been tense since we'd entered the building. For a place he claimed would help him, his actions made me skeptical.

"Are we safe here?" I whispered.

He leaned closer until his lips nearly brushed my ear and I could feel his breath on my cheek. A tingle shot through me to the floor. "You are never safe with the fae." He paused and sighed. "I wish you had stayed with the witches."

"Then who would have held your sword?"

Aengus pulled back and lifted an eyebrow. I yanked my hand free of his and waved it furiously. I'd meant the words seriously, remembering the moment when Excalibur had fallen to the pavement, but the moment they left my mouth I realized how they could be taken. "I didn't mean like your personal sword. Obviously I meant Excalibur."

"I knew what you meant," he teased. He glanced over at the fae receptionist waiting for us to follow and his face fell. He took a deep breath and looked hard at me. "Stay close."

I gave myself a mental shake as I watched him walk away. Nothing good would come from falling for Aengus. Nothing. I needed to help him fix Excalibur so he could close the veil and I needed to find a way to help Nibs. That's it. Nothing more.

The fae receptionist led us down the gray hallway toward a closed office at the very back. Gold nameplates beside more closed doors ran along both sides of the hall, but I couldn't hear anyone inside. The gold nameplate at the end read only *Aurnia*. The fae receptionist knocked once, then opened the door. With a gesture, she urged us into the room, then exited with a quiet click behind us.

More stark gray walls and uncomfortable furniture mirrored the outside, except a massive cherry wood desk dominated the middle of the room. The fae behind the desk, Lady Aurnia the leader of the Seelie I assumed, at first glance looked like any other professional human woman in a maroon pantsuit, minimal makeup, and a conservative yet well styled hairdo. I wasn't sure I understood the power structure. The Unseelie had definitely been led by the queen, but Theo mentioned voting. Was this fae an elected official?

Lady Aurnia stood slowly, her eyes falling to Excalibur in my hand before they moved to me and then rested on Aengus.

"When Theo mentioned he'd received word from you, I assumed you both would have returned here sooner," she said. Every expression she made was exaggerated. Eyebrows lifted higher than they should, mouth opening wider than was natural. When she spoke, she was terrifying. Instinctively, my hand went to my hoodie pocket to protect Nibs.

"I was unexpectedly waylaid by the Green Knight." As Aengus spoke, he bowed low at the hip.

No one demanded that I bow as well, so I didn't. No need to make a fool out of myself twice in one day.

The Seelie Queen? President? Imperator? Appeared livid. "The Unseelie know of Excalibur?"

"It would seem so, my lady."

She let out a long hum, that sounded almost like a growl. "After a year, I guess it was inevitable." Her gaze hardened on Aengus. "You led us on a merry chase, poppet."

Poppet? Who calls a grown man poppet?

Aengus bowed again, which seriously irritated me. "Apologies, my lady."

Lady Aurnia walked around the desk and stalked over, looming like a bird of prey. "But why is Excalibur in the hands of this human?" She leaned in, sniffing. I tried to lean away. "*Custos*," she said like she'd smelled something rotten. She quickly stepped back and glared over at Aengus who took a step closer, blocking her direct line to me.

"That is one of the reasons we are here," Aengus answered. "It seems the sword has chosen a new master. We need to find out how to reverse it so I may return to my duty and close the veil." He bowed his head. "With your help, of course."

Lady Aurnia rested a hip against the desk. She reached to press a button on the phone. "Betty?" she asked and the woman who'd let us into the building answered. "Please find my son and have him report to me."

"Of course, my lady." The line beeped off.

Lady Aurnia straightened and adjusted her suit jacket. "Having the veil open has been quite a trial. Last month, we extracted a troll living out in an abandoned train tunnel. It had eaten at least five homeless people and killed one of our own when we fought it. And a fire salamander in the Carson River nearly destroyed the whole ecosystem. My subjects upstairs have had to work overtime this last year, quelling all the issues." Here she paused and her focus was fully on Aengus. Her unnatural expression turned predatory. "But I must say, it's good to see you again, my poppet."

The energy in the room shifted and although Aengus didn't move, the tension rolled off him filling the space. "You are just as beautiful as I remember." The words dropped like lead.

Lady Aurnia sighed. "If I didn't have a responsibility to the safety of my people, I might be persuaded to keep you, again."

The corner of Aengus's mouth twitched.

In the diner he'd said the Seelie court had both created him and helped close the veil, but the way she was talking it seemed she personally had had a hand in his creation. Not only would that make her as old as Aengus, but it meant she was the bitch who'd turned him into a vampire.

It felt hard to breathe and I realized every muscle in my abdomen was clenched. "You can't keep him. He's not property." My words started strong but fizzled to barely a whisper when Lady Aurnia swung her attention to me and lifted an eyebrow.

Aengus turned and patted the air. That's when I realized I'd raised the sword unconsciously. I dropped the tip toward the floor, but I kept glaring.

She just laughed. The sound like breaking glass. "Actually, mongrel, he is." She paused for a moment, cocking her head as she looked at me. "Why would the sword choose you? What makes you special?"

Now I'd been insulted by both courts. Lucky me. I equal parts wanted to duck my head and hide and at the same time brandish my sword and escape with the knight.

I did neither as Theo burst into the room, his lavender skin and pointed ears on full display without a glamour. "Look who I found, Mother," Theo said brightly. He marched around and grabbed Aengus's neck possessively as he had in the diner, giving Aengus a shake. I could see Aengus hunch slightly. "Took quite a while checking on the girl. Not trying to make me jealous, I hope." Theo appraised me and shrugged. "Or were you offering her up for goodwill?"

Aengus made a noise like a low growl.

Theo chuckled. "I think those years buried made you forget who you are. Merlin's spell might've altered you, but you'll always be a *fola tráill.*"

Like mother, like son. Both clearly saw Aengus as a possession. I clenched Excalibur tighter and tried not to grind my teeth down to nubs.

"Theo, darling," Lady Aurnia said, trying to draw his attention away from Aengus. When he didn't look at her, she clapped loudly. "Theo," she snapped. Theo's hand dropped from Aengus's neck, and he straightened. "Take them to Gaius and report everything that's said." Lady Aurnia walked back around the desk to sit back down.

"Alright," Theo answered. "You heard her, off we go." He swung his hands to herd us back toward the door.

"And Theo," Lady Aurnia called as we stepped back into the hall. Theo turned to her. "Hands off until decisions have been made."

"Of course!" Theo said cheerily and closed the door. The moment it clicked shut, his face hardened. "Let's go," he ordered and took off back toward the lobby.

Everything had happened so fast I hadn't had a chance to ask about Nibs and now I had no choice but to follow. Maybe this Gaius would have answers.

Chapter Fifteen

Aengus followed close to Theo, but I fell behind. My joints ached from exhaustion, and I couldn't make my legs move any faster. They reached the elevator and Theo scowled when Aengus forced him to hold the door until I reached it.

Instead of going up, we went down and the doors opened into a dungeon. Because apparently, my already insane day wouldn't have been complete without one. Sconces flickered their light against the walls and low ceiling. Several corridors branched off from the main circle, which had a low ceiling but was wide. It made me think of a great hall in a castle.

The short elevator trip had made me queasy. I leaned up against the cool stone wall and pressed my cheek to it. I looked at the sconce above me and realized it was electric. A fake fabric flame trembled over a small fan.

This was ridiculous. If not for the little ball of Brownie curled in my hoodie pocket, Excalibur and I would be out the door. I lifted the sword in front of my face. Why did it even want me? It made no sense. I sighed under the weight of it all.

Theo heard me and assumed the sigh was judgmental. He

puffed up his chest and crossed his arms. "My mother is all about the modern world, but she does miss her medieval days. When she found out some molekin up in Tahoe were building tunnels for the mob, she hired them to dig here. Some visitors even like these rooms better. Underground, closer to Underhill."

I'd heard of the tunnels under the casinos up in Tahoe, but I'd never heard of molekin, although I could guess by the name why they were good at making tunnels. Dennriall had mentioned Underhill at the Unseelie Court, too. I was well aware how little I still didn't know. If I had the strength, I'd have asked about it. Instead, I just leaned.

Aengus looked over his shoulder and saw me. He rushed back, brow furrowed.

"What's wrong with her?" Theo demanded.

"I'm okay." I pushed myself away from the wall. I smiled reassuringly at Aengus, but he still looked concerned. "Really, I'm okay." But even as I stood there, I could feel the walls pushing inward and the ceiling falling toward me. It took all my strength to start walking again.

"She is human. She will need to eat and rest soon." Aengus said sharply to Theo's back.

"We see Gaius first." Theo called over his shoulder as he started down one of the offshoot tunnels.

"Are you able?" Aengus asked.

I nodded. "I just need to get moving. I'll be fine."

He didn't look as if he believed me and stayed close as we started forward.

The fake flame sconces were also motion activated and after a few feet, all of them lit up and down the new tunnel in a wave. Aside from the sound of the fake wicks snapping, the corridor was almost oppressively quiet, and there was a sharp smell of bleach in the air. The sound of screams and chains might have been less creepy.

"Anguselus, come up here," Theo called back to us. Aengus

looked hesitant, but I encouraged him to go. At the moment, keeping Theo happy seemed like the right move. I fought the urge to run up and push myself between them when Theo pulled Aengus in close.

Who was I kidding, I couldn't run even if an *ossorian* appeared. I shuffled on and fell farther and farther behind until Theo and Aengus were nearly to the end where the tunnel branched once more. I stumbled to a stop to rest a moment. I debated putting down the sword. My hand gripped the hilt tighter at the thought, so I didn't. From a dark alcove near me, someone whispered "Help me." I spun to face the shadows, but I couldn't see anyone. I stepped closer.

"Help me," the voice whispered slightly louder.

I thought about calling Theo and Aengus back, but instead stepped toward the alcove. It led to an open doorway and as my eyes adjusted, I could make out a room in the darkness. No electric sconces switched on. I made sure Nibs was centered in my pocket, then removed my phone to use the flashlight. The battery was in the red. Unlike the astringent bleach smell in the hallway, the room smelled musty and forgotten, and a layer of dirt covered everything. I could make out a bed with a bare mattress, a tall dresser, and a small table with one chair. As the light passed over the chair, something glinted on the floor.

Curious, I walked closer and crouched down to see it better. It was a bracelet. One of the kind you slip over the wrist. I set Excalibur under my arm and reached out for it. When I stood up with the jewelry in my hand the flashlight lit the corner.

A woman, translucent and barely formed floated in the corner.

I screamed and stumbled backwards. Excalibur clattered to the floor. I looked down at the dropped sword, then back toward the corner. The woman was gone. A ghost? But I'd never seen one so insubstantial. The ghosts, even the older ones at the museum, always looked solid to me unless I tried to touch them.

"Imogen!" Aengus called from down the hall. I could hear his running footfalls racing toward my direction.

"I'm fine," I called as I shoved the bracelet and my phone in my rear pockets and grabbed Excalibur from the floor. Putting a hand on Nibs, I turned to leave the room — and found myself returned to the alcove with nothing but a wall behind me. I spun in a circle. No room. I reached out and ran a hand over the stone. My fingers scraped across the cool, rough surface. How was that possible? An illusion? A hallucination due to my severe lack of food?

Aengus rushed into the shadowed nook and expelled a sigh that sounded like relief. Part of me wondered, what wasn't he telling me if my mere rest stop had him worried? He stepped close, his arms out in front of him as if he was going to pull me into his embrace. I found it hard to breathe as he intently looked me over. I wanted to step closer.

I took a step back, instead.

"I'm fine, really. There was a room, but it's gone now..." I tailed off as I looked over my shoulder. "I thought someone needed help."

Aengus placed a gloved hand on my arm. I looked from his hand to his face. "Imogen, the Seelie have many ways in which to lure you in. Trust nothing and no one here. Do you understand?" He looked genuinely upset, frightened even. "Please tell me you understand?"

I wanted to rest my hand on his stubbled cheek and comfort him. I squeezed the hilt in my hand and nodded.

Theo appeared behind Aengus. "What's the holdup? I don't plan on spending my whole evening down here."

"We're coming." Aengus dropped his hand from my arm and I felt its loss. Theo stomped off, not checking to see if we followed. Aengus gestured for me to go first. With one last look at the wall that had definitely been a room, I moved forward, Aengus right behind me.

Exhaustion covered me like an overzealous weighted blanket and emotions I might have been able to keep in check, were an inescapable avalanche. Fear for Nibs was the heaviest of all. I kept placing my hand inside to check that she breathed. What if she never woke up? Tears pricked at my eyes. I slowed until I was even with Aengus, keeping my voice low, I asked. "Do you think the Seelie can help Nibs?" He eyed my hoodie pocket for a second before looking straight ahead and didn't answer right away. I felt cold inside.

"I cannot say," he finally answered.

My hand against the Nibs' lump-like form trembled, as I tried to calm my doubts.

At the end of the corridor, Theo stopped at a wooden door, the kind you find in castles and dungeons. Finding someone to handcraft it must have cost a fortune, but I guess there was always magic. Theo knocked and a moment later the door swung inward. We all stepped inside — straight into a beachfront bungalow.

Through an open wall leading to sand and palm trees, water lapped against the shore in gentle waves, The sun shone so bright I squinted. It had been evening when we'd arrived at the Seelie Court, but the midday sun illuminated everything. Cushioned rattan lounge chairs in a half-moon formation invited us to recline and relax.

"Gaius," Theo bellowed.

A voice called jovially from a hallway off to our side. "Take your shoes off. Let your toes stretch." A wizened fae, Gaius I guessed, entered the main room. He stood tall with spindly arms and legs and eyebrows the size of small birds. A long white beard nearly reached his white shorts and covered much of the front of his pineapple-patterned shirt. A pair of sunglasses sat on top of his long white hair. He looked like a combination of wizard, elf, and beach bum. He pointed out into the sunshine. "The sand is nice and warm today."

"How? I don't... it doesn't make any... There's beach." I stumbled over my words. Hunger and exhaustion were really making it hard to focus.

"It's not really a beach. It's a memory," Gaius started to explain.

"It's a stupid waste of magic is what it is," Theo interrupted, coming back toward us.

Gaius snorted. "If I'm forced to follow the Seelie Court all over this realm, I at least get to pretend I'm somewhere I like."

Gaius seemed to notice Excalibur for the first time. He reached out and Aengus stepped in between, blocking him. Gaius considered Aengus for a moment but then turned his gaze to me. "You, girl, are holding a very important sword."

"Yes," I agreed.

Theo reached over and grabbed at Excalibur's hilt. "The queen wants to know what's wrong with Excalibur." He pulled the sword roughly toward him. I could have told him what would happen, but I got a lot of pleasure out of just letting go. The sword immediately fell from Theo's grip to the floor with a heavy thud. I smirked at his confusion and Aengus almost cracked a smile.

"Idiot," Gaius said and Theo turned red and scowled.

Gaius seemed to bend completely in half as he lowered himself to get a closer look at the sword on the floor. He ran a hand along the blade and let out a low hum. "This isn't Excalibur," he said as he stood back up.

Aengus shook his head. "You are mistaken, sir."

"What I mean is, that is *no longer* Excalibur." Gaius looked at me. "Pick up the sword, please." I did as he asked. He crossed his arms. "What is your name, miss?"

Remembering Aengus's warning, I looked at him, unsure what to do. He nodded so I answered the question. "Genny Wylde."

"Then the sword is now the Wylde Sword."

"What?" I squeaked. "That can't be right." I looked at Aengus. But Aengus wasn't looking at me, he was staring at the sword. His fists clenched at his sides, the leather threatening to burst along his knuckles. "I didn't do this," I pleaded to him.

Gaius pulled the sunglasses from his head and placed them on his nose. "I'm not wrong. Now I'm going to go back to my nap in the sun. If you'll excuse me."

"Wait," Both Theo and Aengus demanded.

Gaius paused.

"How do we change it back," Aengus asked, tightness in his voice.

With a finger, Gaius pushed his sunglasses down far enough to see over them. "You can't. The sword chooses its destiny. No force can change that."

Aengus took a step closer. Gaius towered over Aengus, but it was Gaius who seemed to shrink under Aengus's energy. "I must return to the tomb. I am to close the veil, that is *my* destiny, my *only* purpose. How am I to do that without Excalibur?" The tightness in Aengus's voice turned to desperation.

His only purpose? That didn't seem right. No one should be desperate to return to a tomb.

Gaius stroked his beard. "Possibly a new sword could be forged with the purpose of being a key. You would need to speak with a druid. That skill is beyond me."

"Maybe if you didn't use all your magic on this illusion, you'd be more help." Theo snapped. "Let's go." He gave Aengus a push against his chest. Aengus didn't move and Theo's eyes widened in surprise. Aengus ignored him and continued to focus on Gaius.

"The druids are extinct. How do we go about finding something that does not exist?" Aengus asked.

Gaius pondered the question and seemed hesitant in his answer. "There was a druid who followed the courts as they moved. The last I saw of him was Greece, but it's possible he followed the courts here. That's all I know."

Aengus nodded and turned to leave. Gaius turned from us to exit out onto the beach.

"Wait!" I screeched louder than I'd meant to. Everyone stopped and stared at me. I tried not to allow their focused attention to make me nervous. I set the sword down across the arms of a nearby rattan chair and reached into my hoodie. Gently, I pulled Nibbleink out and held her balled form up for Gaius to see. "Can you help her?"

Gaius blinked, then leaned in. "A Brownie?"

Theo grumbled with impatience behind me. I ignored him. "She touched the axe of the Green Knight. I'm told she'll die." I barely got out the words. All the times I'd complained to myself about all the money and stress Nibs had caused seemed trivial. I couldn't lose her.

"I'm sorry," Gaius started, and I wanted to scream "no!" in his face. "The axe was made by a Cailleach fae. I have no power to reverse its affects."

A cailleach fae? That was what Jane said I was, but even though I supposedly had magic, I had no idea how to access it. Or what to do with it if I did. Maybe there was someone like me who could help Nibs. "Where can I find one?" I asked.

Gaius shook his head. "None alive that I know of." He must have seen the despair on my face because his expression softened. "Here, leave your little friend with me for a bit. Maybe I can find a way to slow the magic." He reached out with cupped hands. I looked at Nibs, so vulnerable and I pulled her closer to me.

Aengus moved to my side. "Gaius, do you swear you mean no harm to this Brownie?"

Gaius nodded and patted his beard. "I swear I mean no harm to this Brownie and only wish to help. It's a much nicer project than what I'm normally forced to work on."

Theo huffed behind me. "Can we go now?"

I looked at Aengus one more time for assurance. He nodded and gestured toward Gaius who reached out his cupped hands once more. I let Nibs go, the absence of her tiny body was a heavy weight on my heart.

I couldn't move.

Gaius cradled Nibs against his chest with one hand, his beard almost lying over her like a shroud, and gestured with the other. The beach house disappeared. Taking with it the sound of the waves and the smell of salt and sun-heated sand. Now we stood in a bland apartment — utilitarian and cold. "I'll start now to help your friend."

I pursed my lips trying to keep tears from falling. "She's family," I whispered. Gaius acknowledged my words with a nod.

"Come," Aengus said softly.

I reached over and grabbed Excalibur — no, the Wylde Sword? — from the chair, no longer rattan and inviting but as stiff as the chairs in the lobby from earlier and followed the men out of the room.

Chapter Sixteen

Theo walked slower on the return trip back to the elevator. "My mother isn't going to like this. That bastard was no help. Is his day ruined because the veil's open? No, he gets to lie on a beach. I'm the one that has to go handle the trolls in tunnels and the salamanders in the river."

"We will figure this out," Aengus said, but his words sounded hollow.

"Fuck all," Theo swore, ignoring him as he slammed a fist against the stone. His anger fell flat for me. He sounded less like someone concerned that the open veil would let more dangerous fae through and more like a spoiled kid being forced to work.

We continued in silence.

Every step we took away from Gaius made me question my decision. Had leaving Nibs been the right call? Wouldn't she be safer with me? But logically I knew that any help Gaius could provide meant I had longer to find a true solution. Maybe even long enough to reclaim my magic and help her myself. I had no idea if any of that was even possible, but I wouldn't let myself entertain the possibility of failure.

The sword was heavy in my grip. Heavy in the sense that I was exhausted. Holding anything would have been hard. I wished I could take a break and hand it to Aengus. But I couldn't because the sword was... mine? Why would a sword choose me? Aengus walked a few strides in front of me, his long coat pulling against his back and flowing out from around his legs. The better question — why would the sword choose me over someone incredibly strong and blindingly devoted to his cause? It didn't make sense at all.

The elevator brought us back up to the first floor. Betty stood, waiting as we stepped out. "Lady Aurnia has asked me to show you to your rooms for this evening. Dinner has been provided and she will speak with you both in the morning."

"We're staying here?" I whispered sharply, leaning close to Aengus. Leaving Nibs with Gaius was one thing, I was trying to save her life, but staying in this place set off all my alarm bells.

Aengus shifted until he blocked me from both Theo and Betty. He kept his voice low, but his eyes spoke volumes. I wasn't safe. "No, you must leave Excalibur and go home. You have put yourself in enough danger. I will alert you if there is a change with the Brownie."

Leaving Aengus behind didn't lessen my alarm.

Aengus spun around when Betty stepped closer and shook her head at his suggestion. "The Seelie Court has formally extended the invitation to Miss Genny Wylde. She stays at the behest of its leader."

That sounded ominous. And I could see Aengus visibly tense.

"I can't leave, can I?" I asked. Aengus didn't look my way, only shook his head in answer.

Betty cast her bored gaze on Theo. "Your mother wishes to speak with you now. She's in her quarters."

Theo gripped Aengus by the arm. "I know you don't need my blood anymore, but I'll come by later anyway." Aengus dipped his head, his jaw so tight I could almost hear his teeth grind.

Blood. The word shocked me. Aengus had told me what he was

before Merlin had altered him, but hearing Theo blithely mention the need made it one hundred times more sinister.

I wanted to step between them. I thought about those scenes in movies and books where the vampire or werewolf says "The woman is mine" to keep her safe. Aengus wasn't mine and I certainly wasn't a vampire or a werewolf with the strength to back up those words, even with a sword, but unrealistic as it was, the desire to protect him rose up strong and intense within me.

Theo let go of Aengus's arm and walked away. I only thought I was imagining poking Theo with Excalibur when I felt Aengus's hand gently push the raised sword back down toward the floor.

"Shall we go?" Betty asked, gesturing back toward the elevator.

As if I had a choice. I sent a longing look toward the exit before I answered. "Yes, let's."

Betty led us back into the elevator and up to the third floor, which felt more like a fancy hotel than an office building. "Do all the Seelie live here?" I asked as we walked down the black marble hallway with chandeliers every few feet.

"No," Betty answered. "Only Lady Aurnia and her closest advisors live at court. We also keep rooms available for guests."

I snorted at the term guests. More like prisoners.

She stopped at a door and keyed in a code. Her fingers moved too fast for me to remember it. She pushed open the door and gestured for me to enter. I took a step in. "Dinner has been set on your table. Aengus, your room is further down the hall."

She made to shut the door, but I jumped out before it closed. "I won't stay in this room by myself." She opened her mouth to protest, but I continued. "I won't. I'll leave and take Excalibur with me. Then how will you all close the veil?" Words were just pouring out of my mouth, but I knew Aengus shouldn't be left alone. Not here. And I definitely didn't want to be alone.

Aengus paused for only a moment, scrutinizing me, before he moved toward me. "It seems I should stay. The human appears distressed." Betty hesitated. "I'm sure Lady Aurnia would not hold you responsible if she has to use resources to find the human if she runs, but... " He trailed off and didn't continue.

Betty huffed and rekeyed the pad to open the door. Both Aengus and I walked in, before she quickly pulled it closed.

Now Aengus and I were in the room together — alone.

We both smiled nervously.

The furniture looked only slightly more comfortable than the chairs in the lobby. The same monochromatic color scheme played out across a two-piece sectional with a chaise lounge on one end and a tiny table with chairs next to an even tinier kitchenette and one lone bed. I nearly laughed out loud. Of course, there was only one bed. The closed door next to us was likely the bathroom. "You should eat," Aengus said moving toward the table. He lifted the metal cover off one of the plates.

The smell hit my stomach so hard I nearly bowled over, but instead of walking toward the food I turned back toward the door and pulled on the latch. Locked. I had expected that but had to try. Then I set Excalibur — it was just easier to keep calling it that — on the floor across the bottom of the door.

I caught Aengus's eye. "I have a theory." I didn't elaborate.

Aengus lowered the lid back onto the plate and looked at me hard. "You should not have stayed." I smirked at the implication that I wasn't forced. "Fair point, but I should have distracted them — fought them — so you could get free."

A realization I'd been slowly forming solidified at his words. "Can a person like me," I wasn't ready to call myself *custos*, "really ever be free of the fae?"

Aengus made a frustrated sound and pursed his lips. "Another fair point."

Part of me wondered if Aengus had created a distraction would I have taken the out. Nibs was still down in the dungeon and I couldn't seem to stop worrying over the unsettling dynamic going on between Aengus, Theo, and Lady Aurnia.

Aengus dropped the discussion and lifted another cover off a plate. "There's enough here for both of us."

I moved to the table, trying hard not to drool. I was so hungry my brain was having trouble focusing, but I remembered something important. "Nibs told me I should never eat food offered by a fae."

Aengus nodded at my words. "Your Brownie is correct, but this is purely human food. No fae magic involved."

I couldn't deny my hunger any longer and pounced on the first thing I could reach. Bread never tasted so delicious.

Even though there had been plates of food and a full basket of bread, in no time only crumbs remained. I slid off the chair and groaned as I dropped down onto the sectional, my full stomach zapping all my strength. Aengus got up as well, but he made his way to one of the two drawered bedside tables. He opened the top drawer and made a satisfied grunt. He reached in and pulled out a bundle of silky cream fabric that flowed between his gloved fingers.

He walked over and held out the bundle to me. "Here. They are night clothes. The Seelie are all about comfort."

I reached out for the pajamas and felt their cool silkiness slide down into my palms. I rubbed the fabric between my fingertips. Real silk, for sure.

"You can use the shower first if you want." For a moment, Aengus looked sheepish. "I tend to use up all the hot water. I have not quite gotten used to the novelty."

I laughed. "I'll try not to be too long."

I stood up only to realize how close that made our proximity. It seemed to keep happening with us.

Aengus still hadn't replaced his shirt and I couldn't help but follow with my eyes the striated lines of his abs up toward his chest. My fingers twitched with the desire to touch and a bloom of warmth settled in my chest. I jerked my gaze to his face hoping for calm. Instead, his golden eyes dilated and sent my heart pounding until I could barely breathe.

The moment ended when Aengus turned his head to the side,

his expression tight and unreadable. I was reminded that in his position he inherently didn't have a lot a of choice and I had forced him to remain with me. "I put you in a tough spot when I insisted you stay with me. I'm sorry."

Aengus closed his eyes and sighed, before he turned his face back to me. "There is guilt to share. As I said before, the *custos* gave me family. A place to belong. I feel that when I am near you. Being here is dangerous for you, yet I am glad for your company. It is selfish." His eyes followed the curve of my neck and down my arm. Gingerly, he pulled my fingers into his gloved palm. "I have been alone for a very long time."

My pounding heart squeezed in empathy. Logic fought through the haze of heat and I reminded myself I had only known the man for two days. I was basically in a hotel room with a stranger. A stranger who had admitted to being dangerous. A stranger that possibly needed blood.

Desire fizzled — or tried to. I didn't want to admit that I'd been feeling a connection while surrounded by the fae. Almost as if I suddenly had found the place where I fit in and being close to Aengus made me feel it most of all.

I tried to step away, but Aengus stepped back first. "You should shower."

Afraid of what I would say if I opened my mouth, I spun away and disappeared behind the bathroom door.

Under the fall of warm water, my heart slowed and my muscles relaxed to the point I feared I might just fall asleep. But then my brain flooded with everything that had happened in the last twenty-four hours and I remained awake, energy renewed by worries.

My immediate concerns, the vampire sharing my suite and the fact that a sword had 'chosen' me, were nothing compared to my worry for Nibs. I shut off the water and stepped out. Even the warmed plush towel wrapped around me couldn't ease my fears. What if Gaius couldn't help and Nibs died without me there? She was surrounded by strangers. I shouldn't have left her there.

I dried and dressed in the silk pajamas, but I was not ready to leave. I pulled open the vanity drawers and found a variety of individually packaged sundries. I opened a comb and ran it through my hair. Then I opened a toothbrush and toothpaste.

As I brushed my teeth, I noticed a hair dryer still covered in manufacturing stickers, propped against the wall on the counter. As I swished some mouthwash, I picked at the biggest sticker, pulling it off intact. It might just come in handy. I stuck the sticker to the back of my hand.

I thought about picking up my sweatshirt and jeans, but they looked even dirtier lying in a lump on the floor. I bent down and pulled the bracelet I found in the dungeon from my discarded pants. I took a moment to really look at it. The design appeared to be a miniature version of what I'd seen around the necks of celts in illustrations. A torque, I thought it was called. An inscription wove seamlessly into the design, *Tá mo chroí istigh ionat.* I had no idea what it meant, but the whole piece was very beautiful.

As I dropped it into my pajama pocket, I looked up into the mirror. I couldn't stop the scream that leaped out of me. For the briefest moment, the ghostly woman from the dungeon had been in the mirror staring back.

Aengus pounded on the door, demanding to know if I was all right.

I shuddered. "I'm fine," I called, not quite sure if that was the truth. I kicked the pile of clothes farther under the vanity and opened the bathroom door.

Aengus stood near, chest now completely bare, black silk pajamas in hand. Past him, his long coat now draped on one of the dining chairs. Light pink scars covered his left shoulder and traveled down his muscled chest from the *ossorian* attack, injuries that would still be open and raw on anyone else. I scrunched the silk against my abdomen and took a deep breath.

He looked around me, searching the bathroom for what had caused my scream.

Jittery with tension, I stepped out. "I just scared myself. It's your turn, sorry I took so long."

Aengus seemed satisfied that there wasn't anything wrong and said, "I am certain I will take longer," as he passed.

The sticker I'd taken pulled against my skin and reminded me of its possible purpose. I stuck it on the doorframe next to the handle of the exit. I might not get to use it, but I'd watched enough action/spy shows to know that being prepared was the most important part of surviving. Then I settled into the couch to wait for Aengus. I turned on the television but couldn't concentrate on anything so I switched it off.

The face of the woman from the dungeon and the mirror niggled at me. She seemed so familiar. Had she really been there, or was my brain hallucinating? I'd gone through enough the last few days it wouldn't surprise me if my brain was a little traumatized.

The sound of the shower ran for quite a while. I almost knocked on the door to make sure he hadn't passed out when it finally shut off. Not too long after, he came out and a huge billow of steam followed him. Hair still darkened by water was swept back away from his face and the black silk pajamas draped over him like they were tailor-made. Even though Aengus had been practically topless this entire time, there was something very intimate about seeing him walk out of the bathroom damp and relaxed. Realizing I was staring, again, I ducked my head. Why had I thought sharing a room would be a good idea?

He didn't speak. He didn't sit down. When I couldn't bear the silence any longer, I lifted my gaze.

Our eyes locked.

Seconds? Minutes? I didn't know how long. My heart beat frantically all the way to the tips of my fingers. Static seemed to tingle over my face and down my neck. I felt very exposed sitting cross-legged on the couch, the big pajama shirt dipping low on my chest. I hastily pulled it up. Without a word, Aengus turned away and walked over to the draped, long coat. He reached into a pocket and pulled out his leather gloves. He walked to the sectional but didn't sit down.

"You don't need to put those on, I'll keep my distance." I tried to give a natural smile and put my hands up in mock surrender.

"But what if I cannot?" he asked, his features serious.

I suddenly felt like I was underwater. I couldn't breathe and sound warbled in my ears. I pulled back, pressing myself deeply into the back of the couch. Not out of fear that his touch would knock me out. My whole body zinged at the thought of his hands on me.

Aengus sat with a heavy sigh, rubbing the back of his neck. "That was meant in jest, but it was poorly done. I am not quite myself."

A joke? Everything was so serious and filled with worry, maybe a little humor would help. I smiled and winked. "I'm sure many a pretty girl was rendered powerless by your charm."

Aengus didn't laugh. Instead, he narrowed his eyes and frowned. "You are strong and beautiful and in another lifetime I would have pursued you," he paused, "but no one should ever be powerless."

So much for lightening the mood. I had an inkling that Aengus had just revealed something very telling, and very dark, about his past. He didn't pull on the gloves though but held them in his lap. I reached for the controller on the table, rethinking my desire to watch something mindless.

"Please, I beg you to leave it off. The pictures move too fast and make my head hurt."

It made sense, but it was a very big reminder that Aengus really was a man out of time, no matter how seamlessly he seemed to fit in. He'd never watched a movie or gone down a rabbit hole of YouTube videos. The digital age was as foreign to him as the Iron Age was to me. I set the controller down.

The soft beeps of the keypad rang out loudly in the silence, followed by the latch jiggling. Both Aengus and I leaped to our feet. My heart pounded in my chest but for a completely different reason this time.

"I can't get in, Aengus. Come open the door." It was Theo. Aengus made his way across the room and I followed close behind. Theo could only open it about an inch until it stopped when it came in contact with the sword on the floor. Just as I had hoped.

Aengus reached for the door handle and pulled. The door refused to open wider. Aengus looked over his shoulder at me. "Imogen, move the sword."

I shook my head no.

Theo pounded a fist against the metal on the other side. "Can you hear me? The door is stuck."

"You must." Aengus snapped, but his eyes didn't look angry, they looked anxious, scared.

I leaned in, near as I could to his ear. "You told me I couldn't trust anyone. Can you be sure that I'm safe if we let him in?"

Aengus scrutinized me. I hoped he couldn't tell that I was less afraid for myself, and more concerned for him. Lady Aurnia had called Aengus property, and Theo's behavior hadn't seemed much better. If Aengus thought he had to protect me, I'd keep him here and maybe keep them out.

Theo threw his shoulder against the door and called for Aengus, who responded, "I am staying with the human tonight. This world is new and unsettling for her." I let out a relieved sigh.

"That's alright, I can help with that," Theo said, his tone cajoling. I thought of what he meant by helping and I was one hundred percent certain I wanted no part of it.

"Please understand, I would open the door, but she is not use to our ways." Aengus leaned in, listening.

I didn't like how deferential he was being. I'll admit, I didn't know Aengus well, but he'd only been confident and in control —

I'd even go as far as to say heroic — in our interactions. In this place, around Theo and Lady Aurnia, he seemed to shrink.

"I'm forced to speak of this with my mother," Theo said, his tone suddenly cold and threatening. I shivered.

"I understand," Aengus responded. He visibly deflated when Theo's footsteps could be heard walking away. He made his way to the couch but didn't sit.

The door remained open an inch. I grabbed the sticker from the wall and slipped it over the latch plate, before closing it. Thank you television.

I moved to where Aengus stood silently. Finally, he looked at me. "I have changed my mind. Play a story on your box. I feel like closing my eyes and listening."

I wished I hadn't told him to leave off his gloves so I could reach out and hold his hand.

Chapter Seventeen

I yanked the bathroom door open and yelled out into the room. "I'm not wearing this!" I immediately regretted it. The pounding in my head that had started to dull returned. A fae mini fridge filled with tiny bottles of alcohol that restocked itself was a dangerous thing. Ask me how I know.

Breakfast and a bag of clothes had been delivered in the early morning by two short and bulbous creatures dressed only in vests and bow ties, one pushing a handcart. They'd efficiently removed last night's dinner and replaced it with more covered trays, dropped a large handled paper bag on the floor beside a chair, then left without saying a word.

My stomach rebelled against anything more than a piece of toast. Aengus, however, annoyingly downed all his and half of mine. Did fae vampires not get hangovers? After we ate, we dumped out the bag of clothes.

I hadn't ever loved the medieval costume look and my feelings for it only soured more when I put on the double-layered white dress. The completely useless silk slippers remained on the bathroom tile. Instead, I went with my docs. Under all the fabric, who would know? I swatted a bell sleeve away so I could yank up the overly flowy linen skirt and not fall on my face as I walked out. "How did anyone move in this?"

Aengus stood by the couch. He didn't look up as he adjusted the belt resting on his hips. The ease of which he handled the apparel drove home my earlier realization of just what a man out of time he was. The clothes fit him in more than just size.

"At least your dress only goes to the knees." I huffed.

"It is called a tunic," He corrected as he looked up. His hands paused in the mid movement of adjusting the cloak draped over one shoulder. His eyes widened. "You are enchanting."

All my frustration floated away under his gaze. Charming words about my looks shouldn't have made my heart stutter, but they did. It wasn't like I was getting praise left and right. Even the art major I dated in college, my only boyfriend, had saved his compliments for other artists not history major nobodies. I dropped the skirt and even brushed it as if to get out the wrinkles. I still didn't like the dress, but being called enchanting wasn't bad. "Thanks. I like your... umm... tunic."

We smiled at the same time.

Aengus walked closer and I held my breath. But he only went to grab his gloves sitting beside an empty plate at the table. While he pulled them on, I bundled all my hair up into a ponytail. "Did the dress arrive with jewelry?" Aengus asked, just as I finished twisting the tie. I touched the bracelet around my wrist.

"This? No, I found it."

"Found it? Where?" His casual tone turned cautious.

"Yesterday in the dungeon."

Aengus reached out, gently grabbing my hand, pulling it closer to scrutinize the bracelet. "You should trust nothing of the fae."

He turned the metal around my wrist and tingles ran up my arm causing me to shiver. His gazed lifted, slowly moving upwards. For a moment he lingered on my lips. I sharply drew in a breath. He sighed heavily in response as his eyes finally found mine. I was reminded of his words from last night. How he's said he been lonely for a long time.

"Was there someone... special? Someone you left behind?" The question was out before I could stop myself. Part of me wanted to tell him not to answer, that the question was rude, but I couldn't.

Aengus smiled softly and his eyes looked glassy. He nodded. "Elaine of Shallot. She died before I was entombed."

Elaine? Like the Lady of Shallot? Then that would mean... oh! "I'm sorry." I whispered.

"I was angry with her at first, but later I understood her sadness was not something I could control." Aengus dipped his head and imperceptibly the space between us narrowed. He reached up and tucked a lock of hair that had escaped my ponytail behind my ear. "Thank you for last night." His voice sounded rough.

I smiled. "It was nice." It had been more than nice. I'd never sat with someone without any fear that I needed to watch what I said or did. My relaxed state last night made it glaring how tense my normal existence was.

Someone knocked at the door.

We jumped apart, my hands releasing Aengus's tunic I'd unconsciously grabbed. What part of "no touching" was I not getting?

"That was close," I said with more lightness than I felt.

Aengus ran a gloved hand over his face and nodded.

From outside the door, the keypad beeped. Aengus walked toward the door just as it opened, and Betty entered, a tablet tucked under her arm. I cursed under my breath that I'd left Excalibur propped against the wall after breakfast had arrived and not in front of the door.

Betty scanned the unused bed, divested of pillows and the top blankets, to where the pillows and blankets had ended up on the sectional. "I hope you both slept well." Her tone implied she didn't believe it possible.

Last night, after Theo left us in peace, we watched a marathon of *The Vampire Diaries*. A little on the nose, but it had seemed a humorous choice. The mini fridge magic was discovered not too long into the marathon. After three shot bottles of Sailor Jerry's, I had turned to Aengus. "If you're a vampire, how can you be out in the sunlight?"

Aengus downed his fifth bourbon and looked down at the tiny bottle. "This is much smoother than what we drank. Is it just American alcohol or is it all better? I think I will try another." He heaved himself back to the mini fridge. He grabbed a handful of different kinds, the bottles clinking together, and plopped back down. He opened a flavored vodka and brought it to his lips. He stopped before drinking it. "You asked me something, about sunlight, was it?"

On the television, one of the vampire characters sizzled in the daylight for emphasis. "You obviously don't do that," I said motioning toward the screen.

He laughed and threw his head back as he took the shot. His whole body shuddered. He set the empty vodka one far away from the five empty bourbons. "Definitely not all good," he said to the bottle then turned to look at me. "Before Merlin's spell sunlight drained me, but immolation was not a concern."

We sat in silence, watching the screen. Before the next episode started, I knocked back a fourth little bottle to ask my next question. Liquid courage. I wasn't sure I even wanted to know the answer. "You don't need to drink blood at all now? Not since Merlin changed you?"

At first, I didn't think he heard me. He remained facing away, quiet. Then slowly he reached over and rolled up his silk sleeve on the arm closest to me and showed me the underside. A red and raised scar wove in a spiral with a line through the middle. I stifled my instinct to run my fingers over it. Finally, he looked at me.

"That is the mark of the Honeythorn. Theo and Lady Aurnia's house. All *fola tráill* are marked and only the blood of that house can sustain. Before Merlin's spell if I did not drink blood from a member of the Honeythorn line, I would have become a beast killing all those around me. A small sip a day kept me hungry but pliable." His words were emotionless and yet I could feel the anger simmering within him.

"Why create the *ossorian* and the *fola tráill*?"

"The same reason anyone enslaves another, to have others fight their battles, to do their work, to exert power."

"A slave?" I whispered in horror.

"What else would you call a being who is bound to another with no way of escape? Whose very body is not his own?" He unrolled his sleeve, but I felt I could still see the mark glowing with malice beneath.

His experience was clearly as far from sexy teenage vampire as it got.

Aengus may need Lady Aurnia and Theo to close the veil, but what must it be like to have to be around the very people who bound and abused you. It wasn't right.

Later, we'd passed out on opposite sides of the sectional sometime in the early hours of morning, miniature empty bottles in a hill on the coffee table.

An icepick of pain stabbed through my head as a reminder and dragging me back from last night's memories.

"We slept well, thank you," Aengus said to Betty, who smirked.

When I wasn't "interviewing the vampire" last night, I'd been worried about Nibs. The creatures from this morning wouldn't or couldn't speak. Betty might be more help. "Do you know if Gaius was able to help Nibs?"

Betty raised an eyebrow. "Nibs?"

"Yes, Nibs, Nibbleink. She's a Brownie."

The fae receptionist screwed up her nose at the word Brownie. "You'll need to speak with Gaius." She turned her gaze from me, clearly a dismissal, and looked to Aengus. "Your presence is requested."

Aengus nodded and moved to follow. I stepped forward to join. Betty raised her hand to stop me. "Your presence is *not* required."

"What?"

Aengus looked shocked as well. "She wields Excalibur," he reminded Betty.

"That is known, but she is to stay here."

Aengus returned to my side. "Then I stay as well."

Betty didn't respond but clicked and swiped on her tablet. When she finished, she looked up with a bored expression on her face and just stared at us both.

"What's going on?" I asked under my breath.

Aengus canted his head slightly. "I do not know."

Minutes ticked by and Betty didn't move. If she hadn't blinked, I'd have thought she was frozen. Finally, the door to the room opened and Lady Aurnia waltzed in flanked by two large fae that looked exactly like Trell from the Unseelie court right down to the secret service get up and dark sunglasses. "This isn't like you, poppet. You're usually better behaved," she said to Aengus.

I cringed at the word "behaved" as if Aengus were a dog or a child. I hated even more that Aengus bowed in deference. "It is my duty to close the veil. I only wish to complete the task as quickly as possible. For that Imogen's help is needed."

Like a striking snake, Lady Aurnia latched onto Aengus's arm and ripped back his sleeve to reveal the mark beneath. "Your duty is whatever I say it is."

The mark may not require Aengus to feed on blood anymore, but Aurnia's touch clearly affected him. He seemed unable to move or break free.

"Let him go," I snapped before I could think better of it.

She gripped Aengus's arm harder and he cried out and fell to his knees. She glared down at him. "Charmed your way into the mongrel's heart? Did you forget you came to me begging to make you forget your pain? That mark was of your own free will and your heart is mine."

I felt sick. Aengus had asked for the mark? That didn't make sense. Not after how we talked last night. No way he would have asked to become a slave. I was missing something.

Lady Aurnia yanked Aengus to his feet. "You will come with me or I kill the girl. Make your choice."

I wanted Aengus to look my way, to give me some sign or explanation, but he didn't. He bowed his head and walked out with Lady Aurnia still gripping his arm, leaving me behind. The two trell clones and Betty followed.

Shock held me rigid as I heard the door snick shut. What the hell had just happened? A swirl of anger, fear, and confusion beat against my rib cage like a trapped bird. I was beginning to believe I was a part of this world. I couldn't deny how it seemed my fae blood was sending roots down through my feet to keep me connected, maybe to Underhill or maybe to Innisfail itself.

Anger fast and hot exploded in every part of me at the memory of Lady Aurnia controlling Aengus. The connection or not, the fae world was just as dangerous as Grandpa had warned and if I didn't get my shit together not only was I likely to die, but Nibs and Aengus as well. I needed to find them both so we could flee and regroup.

Excalibur tipped against the wall seemed to gleam in response. I grabbed her up and pressed my eye to the peephole then pressed my ear to the metal. I saw and heard nothing. I retrieved my phone from the nightstand. A selection of chargers had also been found in the drawers. I shoved it, now fully charged, down my shirt and into my bra. I grabbed the sword and pulled on the door. It came away easily, the blow dryer sticker still covering the latch.

Gold star for me!

Poking my head out, revealed an empty hallway in both directions. It was hard to tell if Lady Aurnia had led Aengus to a different room or even floor. I shuffled out and nearly face planted when my dress caught under the toe of my boot. Gah! I hated dresses! Hopefully, I wouldn't need to run.

Bunching up as much dress as I could in one hand, sword in the other, I made my way to the next room.

Aengus could be behind any one of the doors. I leaned close to listen. All I could hear was my own heartbeat in my ears. The elevator dinged at the end of the hall. Panicked, I threw myself behind an overly large potted plant. Through the leaves, two trells exited the elevator and headed straight to my room. They entered the code and went in. A moment later they were back in the hall. One touched his modern earpiece and proceeded to have a one-way conversation. "She's not in the room, my lady. No, it's just empty. Copy that."

The muscle who'd spoken turned to his partner and indicated he was to guard the door before he turned to head back toward the elevator.

"Ow!" I involuntarily screeched yanking my hand away from where it had rested on the lip of the pot. A limb of the plant snapped back as a seedpod like head hissed through a serrated mouth. I popped the side of my bleeding palm between my lips. Only afterwards did I wonder if the plant was poisonous, but by then the twin trell had turned in my direction.

"Hey!" they cried.

I guess I was going to see if I could run in my costume after all.

I rebundled the fabric in my arms and took off in the opposite direction. If there was an elevator, there had to be stairs. Of course, I wasn't completely sure the fae were concerned with being up to code with fire safety.

Heavy feet followed.

I neared the end of the hallway and noticed a recessed door off to the side with an exit sign. I slammed into it hard and pushed down on the handle. It gave way onto a landing. Unable to let go of my dress to hold the handrail I leaned into it with my elbow riding along the metal and took the concrete stairs as quickly as I could. When I rounded the first corner, I heard the door open again to let in the muscle.

I jumped the last stairs to the next landing. "Run, Genny!" a woman's voice whispered behind me. I spun around. No one was there and the thundering steps of the two trell grew louder. I turned back to continue down and the insubstantial ghost woman from the basement hovered, blocking my way.

"Go out... this door... the elevator... first floor..." Each phrase seemed to push through a barrier, the tail end louder than the start. Her features undulated from visible to nearly nonexistent, but she seemed concerned. "...Go now..."

I only hesitated for a second, before I grabbed the door handle and dashed out of the stairway.

Cubicles filled the open second floor and the air smelled of burnt electronics and stale coffee. The stairwell door clicked closed and heads, mainly human looking with a few outliers, popped up over the tops of the dividers. What did the fae need with employees?

I saw the elevator across the way and there wasn't a straight shot to it. I ducked my head and hustled along the wall of windows, ignoring the calls of "Miss? Miss? Do you need help? Are you lost?"

A guy with abundant facial hair and curled horns stepped out of one of the cubicles as I neared the elevator. He barely reached my shoulder, and it took me a minute to realize he was only dressed from the waist up in a suit and tie. Below he was covered — barely — by hair over his goat-like legs. In one hand he held a mug with the words "Once you go Satyr you'll never come later" and he pointed at my sword with the other. "You must be new. Weapons aren't allowed on the second floor. You'll have to leave it with security."

"Good to know," I said as I ducked my head. Great, now I could add satyr balls to the rest of the mental pictures I'd love to purge. I pounded the elevator button on the wall. The doors took an eternity to open. I jumped inside the moment they opened wide enough and I pounded the "close doors" button. Heaving, I selected the basement. I know the ghost lady had wanted me to escape, but I wasn't leaving without Nibs or Aengus.

The seconds ticked by as the elevator descended.

Seconds that allowed me to worry about Aengus.

What would he do, what would he allow, to return to what he considered his destiny? I thought about last night, he'd seemed relieved when I'd given him an excuse not to go with Theo. As if he needed someone to give him permission not to accept the abuse. There had to be another way to close the veil.

Nibs could die. Aengus was certainly in trouble. I had a sword and a dress and with both I was useless. Tension coiled my muscles. I'd never punched anything in my life, but at that moment I desired nothing more than for my fist to meet a wall. Or maybe my sword?

I could do this. I just needed to grab Nibs, then save the knight. Easy Peasy...

Chapter Eighteen

I knocked hard against Gaius's door with the butt of Excalibur and continued to pound until he opened it. Gone were the beach shorts and Hawaiian shirt, replaced with a heavy green robe tied with a purple sash. A moonstone set in silver rested against his forehead framed by his upward-reaching eyebrows. I didn't wait for him to invite me in, I just pushed past into the dimness. There was no beach bungalow, just the ordinary room from the end of our last visit visible in the shadows.

Gaius shut the door and snapped his fingers in a showman's flourish. All the lights in the room turned on. "Miss Wylde, I was expecting you." He looked past me and seemed surprised I was alone.

"You were expecting me?" The alarm bells dinged, but I wasn't leaving without Nibs.

"Well... yes... of course. I knew you would wish to know if I was able to help your Brownie." He smoothed his hair and twisted his eyebrows straight.

"Is she?" I could barely say the words.

"She's still with us, but I'm unable to halt the spell. The best I could do was lock her in a sort of stasis. A magical sleep if you will." Gaius walked to a table near the galley kitchen. He carefully lifted a bundled towel from the surface and brought it near. With one hand, he lifted a corner to reveal Nibs still lying curled as she had been when I relinquished her to Gaius yesterday, but now she was deathly still. No breathing. No life.

I bit back a sob.

My bra buzzed and I yelped. Sheepishly, I pulled out my cell phone and saw that Everett had texted, concern touching every word as he asked where I was and if I was okay and insisted I call. He said it was very important. I quickly typed a reply that I was fine and that I'd text again soon before I slipped the phone back away.

I looked at the Nibs bundle. There was no way I could carry the sword and Nibs and still be able to function. "Do you have something I could carry her in?" I asked Gaius. Part of me also wanted to ask to raid his wardrobe to get out of the cumbersome dress, but there wasn't enough time.

"I'm certain I can find something that will work." Gaius set Nibs in the towel onto the seat of a nearby chair and pointed at my hand. "You've been injured."

I looked where he pointed. Blood had dried in a line down my pinky and I could see a number of brown drip marks on the bell sleeve. "A potted plant bit me in the hallway. I didn't realize I was still bleeding."

To be fair, a small cut had been the least of my problems while being chased.

I caught the barest of movement out of the corner of my eye and turned my head just as Gaius grabbed my hand. I tried to pull free. If asked I would describe Gaius as frail, but his hold on my wrist felt like a metal vice. He chanted words in an unknown language. The wound stung and blood started to flow, dripping onto the wood floor.

From far away, I could hear Gaius say, "This is unexpected."

I opened my mouth to yell. No sound came out as my vision narrowed to black. I was barely aware of my body crumpling to the floor.

Then all awareness stopped.

Voices in the dark.

I tried to open my eyes and failed. I couldn't feel them. I couldn't feel any part of me. I just floated in the darkness with the voices.

"It's dangerous to do as you ask," a male voice said. Gaius? It sounded like him.

"That's absurd. She's a mongrel. How can she possibly be dangerous?" I recognized Lady Aurnia's voice easily.

"Not just fae blood, my Lady. If I'm not mistaken she is Cailleach fae. It's never been done," Gaius responded. Dennriall's warning raced through my mind. He'd put himself in danger to keep me safe. But now my secret was exposed; a secret I didn't even know I'd been keeping until yesterday. What would happen now?

"Impossible. There hasn't been a Cailleach fae in centuries. Just start the process, she weilds the sword now and I need my gatekeeper."

"Was the spear retrieved?"

"Yes," Lady Aurnia answered. "Finish up here, then find us so we can proceed."

Darkness deepened, sucking me under until I could no longer hear the two of them. Needles raced under my skin, overwhelming my senses with pain. Inch by inch, I grabbed onto the pain, riding it to conciousness and finally out of the dark.

I tried to roll, but only succeeded at opening my eyes. The blades of a ceiling fan rotated slowy above me. It seemed I was still in Gaius's suite. Not on the floor. My hips and shoulders ached against the hard surface beneath me. A table, maybe.

"I can't move." I whispered in mounting panic and tried once more to locate my limbs and move them. I was about as successful as trying to perform a Jedi mind trick; which meant not at all.

"You lied to me, Cailleach fae," a voice purred against my ear. I tried to turn toward it and only managed to move my head. The movement caused an intense wave of nausea and a cold sweat to expel from every pore. I pinched my eyes closed, taking measured breaths.

"About what?" I asked between breathing in and out.

"Your name." A icy touch seared across my cheek. My eyes flew open. "You said your name was Mira." The White Lady leaned close and trailed a finger across my lips, leaving a menthol like burn in its wake. "But that was a lie, wasn't it, Imogen?" I hesitated. "Don't lie or I won't help you get free."

Free. I tried to move, again. My breaths came faster and faster and I put all my force into moving until I could feel the veins in my head swell. Still nothing. Could the White Lady really help me or was it a trick? "Why am I here?" I growled in frustration.

She straightened, taking the cold with her. "You mean why are you being held?" I nodded. "The inept mage bound you. He left to assist Aurnia. I believe the Seelie want to create a new gatekeeper. Is it true that Excalibur has claimed you?"

I nodded again. Fear constricting my throat. A new gatekeeper? Like Aengus had been? My chest ached with how hard my heart pounded and I couldn't find my next breath. He'd been buried alive. Was that why I couldn't move?

The White Lady leaned close again. The mist of her breath cooled my skin. "You won't be able to break free. Not unless you do as I say." I expelled the breath I'd been holding while I strained. She lifted one side of her lips in a sardonic smile. "I will finish what I started." Those words were whispered as if not meant for me and she disappeared from view.

Cold seeped up from the general area of my arm. I tried to move my neck so I could see lower. I only caught sight of her standing near the middle of the table. The bundle holding Nibs sat on the chair in the background.

The White Lady lifted my arm. I felt her frigid touch, but had no awareness of my arm raising. She twisted the bracelet. Unlike when Aengus had done the same movement, the shivers coursing through me were created by fear and not desire. "This is quite powerful. Where did you get it?"

"I found it," I answered.

She laughed, the sound like icicles colliding. "Oh, I doubt that, but it hardly matters who put this in your path. What matters is how we can use it to unleash your magic."

My magic. The magic that had been sealed away from me. I knew Grandpa had asked the witches out of love. Everything he did was to protect and shelter me, but now I was woefully underprepared for everything that had happened. What might my life have looked like if my magic hadn't been locked away all these years? If instead of ignoring the fae, I'd been taught to protect myself? I probably wouldn't be lying on a table unable to move and Nibs might not be near death. If the White Lady wanted to help me reclaim magic, I had to try. "How do I break it?" My words left me in a rush.

"Witch magic comes from the soul. The soul of the witch. The soul of the earth. But fae magic is blood magic. The Cailleach fae must use both in unison. I will open your vein while you bring forth your soul. You will see the path." Light glinted off a knife made of ice that appeared in the White Lady's hand. "The others will return soon. Shall we begin?"

"Wait, you're going to cut my wrist while I *try* to *find* my soul? What kind of directions are those?"

"I can't provide you with any more than that. You are Cailleach fae and therefore rare and barely understood. If we don't start now, the time to escape will be lost."

I could bleed out and die attempting this. Was death worth the risk? I didn't even know if regaining my power would save Nibs. I had no guarantee that it would even free me. This was ludicrous.

I looked at Nibs rolled up in her blanket. I thought about Aengus at the mercy of Lady Aurnia.

As if I really had a choice.

I took a deep breath. "Okay." I thought about the idiom "here goes nothing," but the truth was I was putting in the opposite of nothing. I had to give everything, because if I failed I'd lose it all.

The White Lady's knife came away bloody. My blood. I hadn't even felt the cut. Then came pain. My wrist burned, the intensity increasing with each throbbing pulse, reaching up and out until my entire shoulder and side ached. What if I couldn't find my soul? I'd die on this table. Black spots danced before my eyes. An ocean of waves rushed in my ears and a weight settled on my chest, threatening to sink straight through me. "Breathe," the White Lady snapped.

I exhaled with a shudder and gulped back in another breath.

Look within," she whispered, her words a cold mist against my cheek.

I took a purposefly slow inhale and exhale and closed my eyes.

It was just dark.

No soul. No magic.

I had made a horrible choice. I was going to die.

"Keep breathing," a new voice whispered. Not harsh or angry, but gentle. The same voice from the stairwell. The same voice from the hidden room in the dungeon. A voice that filled me with safety.

Out of the dark, a shape materialized. The shadows coalescing into the form of a woman. No longer wavering and translucent, but solid. I recognized her.

"Hello, Genny," the woman said as she finally appeared fully before me.

"Mom?" I could barely say the word. My memories weren't

numerous, but I remembered flashes and there were pictures boxed away that I'd found when I was still a kid.

She nodded.

"I don't understand." I could feel tears leaking from beneath my closed eyelids and dripping off my cheeks.

"I want to explain, but there isn't time. Geoffery said casting magic was like letting go and falling inward. Hurry, Genny. You must hurry. Let yourself fall. " I heard her fear in each harried word.

I took another deep breath and imagined myself on a cliff falling backwards, freefalling into the lumin of my inner self. Warmth radiated around me, drawing me into an embrace as cozy as a blanket. I could just sleep. Sink into the warmth and glide into dreams. A swirl of gold rose up in my vision, jerking in every direction like a living being. Waking me up. Soon the gold coelesced into a face. My face. I looked into a mirror reflecting an image of me cast in moving gold.

My soul.

I reached toward the reflection. The reflection reached back.

Our hands touched.

An explostion of gold burst before my eyes and my whole body felt as if it had ripped apart. I screamed as my eyes flew open.

Chapter Nineteen

I sat on the table in the middle of a blast zone.

The White Lady was gone.

So was my mother. Had she even truly been there or did I imagine her? Didn't people suffering blood loss have hallucinations?

My gaze flew around the room. Chairs were broken and overturned. Anything light enough and not held down had flown against the walls. Clearly the spell that had bound me had broken. Did that mean my magic had been released as well? Was that how the room had been destroyed? I did a mental inventory. I didn't feel any different.

I shifted to slide to the edge of the table and cried out as my right arm gave way. What had no doubt been shock, was ripped away and pain hit me like a big grilled truck. I gripped my wrist to staunch the flowing blood, my thoughts fighting to stay coherent, and noticed the whole side of my white dress was red with it.

Awkwardly holding my arm, I scooted and hopped down, holding back a yelp by biting my lip. A tea towel hung on a hook by a tiny one-basin sink and I made for it. With my teeth and my left hand, I managed to tie the towel around my wrist and pull it tight. This time I couldn't hold in my yell.

My gaze settled on one of the overturned chairs. Nibs!

I hurried over, crouching next to the thrown cloth. Nibs still lay curled and unmoving within her makeshift bed, but she seemed uninjured. I was supposed to have my power now. The power of the Cailleach fae. The power to help Nibs, but how? Panic had carved a hole out of my middle and right now the empty space ached more than my injured wrist. I reached out to brush a finger across her head, unintentionally leaving a streak of my own blood across her brow. Gross. Nibs was going to kill me, if she woke up and saw it.

When she woke up.

Waking up. Could helping Nibs be as simple as just telling her to wake up? I looked around at the destruction. In all honestly, as long as Nibs came out the other end okay, I'd bring the whole building down around me. On the table, I had freed myself and possibly released my magic by the simple act of falling inward. I closed my eyes. I focused on Nibs waking up, her black eyes springing open and looking on me again. I let my consciousness sink as I imagined myself falling. Again, gold spun like filigree before my closed eyes, dancing to unheard music.

This time I noticed additional strands of gold flowing from pulsing glowing orbs. Some orbs were close, others seemed far in the distance. I pulled the strands from the closer orbs and sighed as a feeling not unlike drinking cocoa on a cold evening filled me with pleasure.

The entryway door slammed open, breaking my concentration.

I tried to stand, stumbled backwards, tripped on my dress and physcially fell flat on my back. From my angle on the floor, I could see only Gaius's head and shoulders as he ran into the room. He halted when he took in the disaster and the empty table.

I rolled to get up and found Excalibur right where I had dropped it when Gaius had attacked me. My right hand was useless. Or was it? There was no longer any pain, but the towel I'd wrapped around my wrist was stiff with blood. I lifted the sword weakly with my left and stood.

Gaius eyed me with curiosity. "You're free." He looked back at the open doorway, eyeing something beyond the threshold I couldn't.

I didn't respond. Black shadows crowded my vision. Blood loss was taking its toll. I shook my head trying to dispel it.

Gaius took a step forward. "I did as I was commanded. I have no quarrel with you."

I raised the tip of my sword a foot off the floor, but my left hand was too weak to lift it further. With no other choice, I added my right hand and the sword lifted easily without even a twinge of pain."Why are you telling me this?"

Gaius shrugged. "I'm nothing if not pragmatic. By the two dead trell outside my door, I can assume you've regained your power. I tried to warn Lady Aurnia."

Dead trell? I hadn't left the room. Had the destruction of the spell caused it? I remembered the orbs and my stomach soured. Had the strands I pulled caused the trell to die?

I fought the urge to sink to the ground, my mind shying away from the revelation of my actions.

Gaius shut the door quietly and turned back to me.. "The Unseelie are upstairs, demanding we turn you over. I have been sent to kill you instead."

"Kill me?" I stumbled over the words. "Why?" My focused jumped around the room, searching for what, I didn't know, but I was suddenly despesperate to find help. My mother had been here earlier. Maybe she would appear again.

"Lady Aurnia hopes that your death will allow the sword to find a new wielder." Gaius confessed.

Overwhelming weakness rushed over me and this time I let myself fall forward onto my knees. Gaius moved to my side. He knelt and pointed at my wrist draped in the bloody cloth. "Let's see if we can close it up. Blood magic's all well and good until you run out." He laughed at his own joke as he unwrapped the towel.

"No!" I yanked my arm away.

"Oh I'm not going to kill you. Not without securing all that power first." He motioned to encompass all of me. "Lady Aurnia is too hasty."

"That doesn't make me feel better."

Gaius looked pensive for a moment. "I guess it wouldn't, would it." Then he snatched my arm. I tried to pull away, but as before his grip was vice-like. We both looked down at my wrist and found it healed. "Already learned how to heal yourself, I see."

I pulled my wrist close to my chest and shuddered. "I didn't know," I defended. I remembered how good it had felt to pull the strands into me and bile rose in my throat.

"Don't worry, you'll find the excuses come easier the more times you do it." He stood up and his gaze fell on where Nibs lay. "Like how important it was to save your little friend."

I looked over, too just in time to see Nibs sit up and stretch. "Nibs," I cried. She looked up scowling in confusion.

"This is not my bed. Don't like." She lifted her lip in a sneer as she gazed down at the towel and huffed.

A laugh of relief left me, which I quicky tried to play off as a cough when Nibs looked my way. "Next time, I'll demand better accommodations." The little Brownie nodded in agreement.

Gaius wasn't right, there was no excuse for what I'd done, but for a moment I let myself focus on Nibs alive and awake. And I still needed to find Aengus. Magic returned or not, we were at a disadvantage. A tiny voice pointed out that all the fae were just balls of energy and if I reached out I could pull all the strands to me.

No! I shut that thought down, but my body still felt hungry.

The door creaked open and all three of us turned. Two spider legs entered followed by the rest of the legs and torso covered with the familiar tartan. "Dennriall!" I stumbled to my feet.

Gaius dipped his head. "Seneschal."

Dennriall barely acknowledged him as he skittered close. "Are you marked?" He demanded of me, reaching out as if to try and grab my arms.

Marked? I remembered my talk with Aengus and hastily lifted each sleeve. Aside from the healed wound there was no mark. I shook my head. Dennriall sighed in relief and lowered his arms.

Gaius snorted. "Of course not. I have some sense."

"And yet the Cailleach fae was bound here." Dennriall said and Gaius paled. "Your incompetent leader is lucky Mistress Crone warned us of Aurnia's stupidity."

"I tell you, I would not have marked her."

I ignored their bickering, right now I needed to leave. I pulled the skirt of my dress out in front of me and sliced downard with Excalibur. The shimmery fabric split. I set the sword down and yanked on the opening. It ripped all the way around until the entire bottom of the dress came free.

Setting down the sword, I took the large circle of fabric, looking tie-dyed red with my blood, and drapped it across my chest like baby sling. I reached for Nibs who instantly jumped into my hands to reach it. Then I grabbed Excalibur. The room spun for a moment and I leaned heavily on the sword, its point digging into the floor. I only felt slightly guilty about using the famed Excalibur like a cane. "Do you know where Aengus is?" I asked Gaius, blinking away the black stars that heralded the fact that my body wanted to pass out.

He looked surprised. "Dead by now, I expect."

All the air left the room. Dead? No that couldn't be right. There was no way Aengus was dead.

I swung Excalibur closer and leaned on it toward Gaius. "Where is he being held?" I demanded.

"It doesn't matter." Gaius pointed at Dennriall. "He's here to bring you to his queen."

I turned to the spider fae. He nodded. "I was sent to find you."

"How did you even know where to look?"

"Aside from the fact that your unlocked magic could indeed stop me, it is not a bad thing to have a powerful being in your debt." I opened my mouth to argue that I wasn't a powerful being, but Dennriall interrupted me. "Do you wish to save your lover, or not?"

"He's not my lover. I've only known him three days." They were logical words and by all rights they should be true. Three days was not enough time to fall in love, maybe for Disney princesses, but not for normal people. And yet three days had been more than enough time to upend my entire life.

"Well, I don't like him," Nibs added, holding onto the side. Her head barely looked over the edge.

"Well, you don't get a vote." I snapped. She huffed and sank deeper into the fabric sling. I felt immense relief that Nibs was okay, but she was still Nibs.

Dennriall lifted an arm high above his head then slowly let it fall in front of him. As it passed over him his shape wavered and shifted. The form of a spider altered to that of a man, with hair long and black, skin a shiny gray, and two human-like eyes, glowing red in the gloom. "Here this should make everything easier."

I couldn't see anything beneath the new form. No spell seemed to cover him. He seemed truly changed. "That's not a glamour," I said, unable to hide the surprise in my voice.

Dennriall lifted a shoulder in a nonchalant shrug. "The perks of being very old. My shape is my will." He gestured again toward the stairs."Lead on."

"Even changed, you're making me go first?"

"Contrary to what you believe, you are the strongest one here. I concede the lead."

I rolled my eyes and took the first step, gripping Excalibur tightly. With my other hand, I trailed it along the wall. The sides and ceiling pressed close and with each step into the black they only seemed to press closer. What was it with the fae and their desire to live in such claustrophic housing?

"Are two dungeons really necessary?" Panic twinged my voice as I looked over my shoulder at Dennriall.

He nodded. "To reach the ley lines and Underhill it is."

I considered the fact that the Unseelie Court existed in a mine shaft and the answer seemed obvious.

"Of course," Dennriall added, his tone markedly disgusted. "The catacombs also hide the Seelie's sin of keeping human pets."

The stairs were now in complete blackness. My pace slowed as I had to feel out each step before taking it. "You mean like *ossorians* and the *fola tráill*? The fae aren't supposed to have them?"

Dennriall hummed an affirmative.

The stairwell might have been dark, but my mind flashed with pictures of the *ossorians* that had chased me and even the dead *ossorian* with the fence post in his chest. I shuddered. The shadows lightened as a faint blue glow rose from below. I picked up my pace.

Honestly, how could it come as a surprise that the fae abused humans? My foundation had been built brick by brick with the knowledge that the fae were dangerous. "Then why do they still have them, and why does the Unseelie Court have my dad?"

"Your father had a choice," Dennriall answered.

I stopped and swung around to stare at him. Nibs tumbled inside the sling and let out a squeak.

Dennriall looked contrite. "I didn't say it was a good choice, but with the fae those details matter. The Seelie still have their *fola tráill* because of politics. Neither side wants to start a war over the lives of humans."

I rolled my eyes. "How considerate of them."

Turning back around, I took the stairs faster as the blue light gained strength. Finally, we reached the bottom.

Near the low ceiling, round-topped mushrooms branched out in clusters randomly casting their blue glow against the stones. Six dark wooden doors, spaced like wheel spokes, circled the room mimicking the dungeon above. The air stuck to my skin and smelled of damp earth. I was reminded of the Unseelie Court. But under my skin, currents seemed to flow. From fingertip to toes and then back up again, warmth swelled and receded in waves.

I swam in it. Swayed with each rush that coursed through me. It was beyond anything I'd ever felt before. If I reached out and grabbed onto that power I could do anything. Just thinking it seemed to give my mind permission and in an instant I was mentally laying my hand on the multitude of golden threads connected to every living thing, letting them slide through my fingers like locks of hair. I wanted to hold them all, to pull them to me, to let the strands fill me completely until all that remained was magic.

"Genny," my mother's voice called through the desire. "Let go, Genny."

My mother was here. Golden threads spun away like frightened fish as I searched for her and reason returned. I let out a shuddering breath. She'd saved me again. Was she a ghost? A construct of my imagination?

I pulled the fabric of the sling away from me to look within. "Are you okay, Nibs?" She looked away in a huff and crossed her arms. She seemed unharmed.

A hand came to rest on my shoulder, making me jump only to realize it was Dennriall, his eyes questioning. Somehow his human guise was harder to get used to after knowing him in his spider form.

"Underhill is strong down here." My voice struggled to escape my throat and it took a herculean effort to stop focusing inward on the magic that beckoned. Instead I tried to focus on the whispers, jumbled and incoherent wafting from under the doors. Which one held Aengus?

As much as I tried to ignore the magic, one golden strand would not disolve. It lingered in the air twisting and twining, until it disapeared behind the nearest door. Aengus. It had to be. "He's here." I reached out my hand to grab the handle, but couldn't make myself lift it to enter.

Dennriall stepped close. "Genny?"

"What if he really is dead in there?"

Dennriall gently pushed me out of the way. "Look away," he murmured and I did as he asked. I could hear the popping hinges of the door as it swung outward. "Birga, the spear of Fiacha." Dennriall sounded surprised. If that was an expletive, it was the weirdest one I'd ever heard. "He is alive." Holding in a cry of relief, I peered around him.

Shock stole the air from my chest in a huff.

In the middle of the room, shackled at the ankles and hanging from chains by his wrists, was Aengus. His head lulled against his chest, above a spear skewering him through his abdomen. His breathing was loud and labored. Blood dribbled from his lips, but only a small amount blood darkened the cloth around the imbedded spear and a small trickle of it ran down his leg from beneath.

"Aengus!" I cried as I ran to him.

He didn't stir, but his labored breathing intensified. Now that I stood close, the sour scent of sweat and the metallic smell of blood filled my nose. Instinctively, I wanted to put a comforting hand on him, but I couldn't. "Why would they do this?" I asked Dennriall as he came up beside me.

"The spear of Fiacha steals magic. If I were to hazard a guess, I believe they used the spear to pull Merlin's spell from your knight to then transfer to you. Or at least, they would have if you hadn't gotten free."

I stared at Aengus. If the spear now held Merlin's spell did that mean Aengus was no longer affected? Did that mean I could touch him?

Hesitantly, I reached out my hand. Nibs from her sling smacked my arm and Dennriall reached toward me to stop me as well.

"We don't know if the spell has been completely transferred," he reasoned.

I shook off Dennrialls touch and ignored Nibs. Hesitantly, I laid my palm against Aengus's bare arm. A tremor ran through him and his head lifted off his chest. He blinked with glassy eyes until they finally focused on me. "Imogen?" he rasped.

His skin beneath my hand was freezing and I absently rubbed it. "Yes, I'm here."

"Go," he pushed out, his eyes wide with fear. "You... you must go... "

I moved my hand from his arm and reached up until I could set it against his cheek. "I'm not leaving you." He closed his eyes and whimpered, as another tremor shuddered through him and he dropped his head back onto his chest. It was hard to pull my hand away. First I set Excalibur down on the ground. Then I pulled the sling off my shoulder and let Nibs out. "We need to get him down," I ordered.

Nibs threw a frustrated hand in the air, but nodded and Dennriall immediately reached for a manacled wrist.

I reached for the other. The manacles were held only by a pin, not a lock. My hands shook as I tried to wiggle it free. Aengus lifted his head and blinked his eyes. "Shhhh," I reassured. He frowned.

"Are you... well?" he managed to get out.

One nervous laugh tumbled out. I should be the one asking, not him. I nodded, unable to speak. My fingers ached as I continued to pull on the pin slowly inching it free. Finally, it fell to the ground with a ping. I looked at Dennriall, who nodded and pulled his pin free. Aengus fell forward right into Dennriall's arms and as gently as he could he laid Aengus down on the stone floor.

The spear wobbled and Aengus gasped, biting down on a groan. His eyes fluttered closed. For a moment, I panicked, but took a breath when I saw his chest rise. I grabbed his hand beside me. It was still gloved.

"We'll need to remove the spear," Dennriall said gently.

I didn't look his way. Aengus's face was pinched with pain even as he lay there unconscious. I thought about how he'd refused to look at me when they'd taken him away. Had he known they would try and kill him? Deliberately, I pulled at each finger of the glove, releasing the leather until I could pull it off. I tossed it away. I gripped Aengus's hand that finally resembled a vampire — cold and corpse-like. I brought it to my cheek to try and warm it.

"Genny?" Dennriall touched my shoulder and Nibs crawled into my lap.

I nodded and a tear leaked out, running down my cheek and down Aengus's arm. I looked up at Dennriall. "Will he die if we take it out?"

"He'll die if we leave it in," he answered softly and the light behind his red eyes dimmed for a moment.

Nibs scurried off my lap and grabbed the blood soaked fabric we'd used for her sling. She held it up like a gift. "Help?"

I took it from her and tried to smile. "I'm sure it will, thanks."

She acknowledged my gratitude with an imperious nod and moved toward Aengus's face. I watched as she bent near his ear and whispered something, following it up with a pat on his cheek. Then she straightened and settled herself on a lump of fabric near the wall, which I realized was the tartan that Aengus had secured over his shoulder earlier when we'd gotten dressed in the room.

Dennriall positioned himself on Aengus's other side near the spear shaft. "I will pull the spear and you must close the wound."

In a panic, I let go of Aengus's hand and crab-crawled away from him. Metal bands seemed to squeeze my chest. "No, I can't," I pleaded. "Coming down here I almost hurt everyone. I can't control it."

Dennriall moved away from the spear and squatted down near me like he was mullifying a scared kitten. His human eyes shown like the jewels they had been. "I'm not a healer. My skills are not what is needed here. I can't do this, but you can."

If I tried to use my magic, others might die. If I didn't, Aengus would certainly die. Absently, I spun the bracelet around my wrist. "Will you help?" I silently asked, hoping my mother was still close.

It was possible I'd created her out of my need to survive. An imaginary friend to soften the fear of everything that had happened the last few days. Figment or not she had kept me safe down here when I'd nearly drowned in my magic.

"I will try," my mother's voice answered, her voice wispy and insubstantial. I sagged in relief.

I crawled back to Aengus and pulled his head into my lap. I looked down at his bloodless face. Some of his curls lay plastered to his forehead. I ran a hand along his scalp to release them. His eyes fluttered, but didn't open. I'd only known him for three days. How could he feel this important?

"It was the same with your father." I looked up and my mother stood as a spector at Aengus's feet. "It's the Wylde blood in you." She smiled playfully. "We don't fall in love easy, but when we do we fall hard."

Aengus was important, but love? Besides he was over 1,400 years old, I wasn't into older men. My mother sighed and I knew she heard my thoughts. "That young man gave up growing old a long time ago and lost whatever future he might have had. But maybe you can give him a new one."

After all he'd been through, maybe he'd rather move on to whatever was next. My hands tightened on him at the thought of him dying. "It has to be his choice," I said. I searched the faces of Dennriall and my mother, even Nibs and they all nodded.

Gently, I brushed my hand over Aengus's cheek, letting a finger run across his lips. "Do you want to stay?" I asked.

He didn't open his eyes, but he turned into my touch. "Stay," Aegnus whispered against my hand.

"Ready?" Dennriall prompted when he heard the answer. I took a deep fortifying breath. I cringed, but nodded. "You will need to mark him with your blood." He instructed and I realized I had accidentally done that back in Gaius's room with Nibs. I could still see the streak of dried blood on her forehead. I ran my finger along the blade of Excalibur lying near. I hissed as it cut deep. When the blood welled, I touched his forehead.

Dennriall placed both hands on the spear, adjusting his fingers to get a good grip. We locked gazes and I nodded. With a heave, he yanked upward and the spear came away, the metal tip red and dripping. Blood gushed from the wound.

Aengus opened his eyes and screamed. The sound gutteral and horrid, like an animal caught in the jaws of a predator. A death call.

What had we done?

"Hurry, Genny." Dennriall urged throwing the spear down and kneeling close.

In my ear, my mother's voice calmed me. "Focus on only the energy you feel in this room. Block out all the rest."

I closed my eyes and let myself fall into the golden strands. I grabbed at them all, hungry. I needed them. "Block out the rest," my mother's voice broke through sharp with fear. With a cry of my own, I let all the strands go accept for the four in the room. I recognized Nibs' fragile strand and let it go. But Dennriall's was thick and powerful. I grabbed hold tight. Aengus's strand looked ashen, it's golden hue dimmed and nearly gone. I forced all the power I could siphen from myself and Dennriall into his strand until it shimmered brightly.

"Let go," my mother whispered.

Out of the corner of my vision I could make all strands. I could just take a little of their energy, and regain my strength. I started to reach out for them.

"Let go," my mother commanded like a boom in my ears.

I shuddered and released everything.

Heaving deeply, trying to catch my breath. I looked down at Aengus. No blood flowed from his wound. The skin appeared whole. He groaned and shifted in my lap. I let him roll away as he got up on his hands and knees. Dennriall moved out of his way, as well.

He remained on all four and didn't try to stand or even look in our direction. "Aengus?" I asked.

Slowly, Aengus lifted his head and turned his face toward me. His eyes were pinched closed. "Aengus?" I whispered again. His eyes flew open and they were now white and milky, his golden irises gone. He opened his mouth impossibly wide and lunge toward me, snapping like a rabid dog. With a jerk, he fell back unable to reach me with his ankles manacled. Dennriall dragged me further across the stone out of his reach.

Numb, I huddled next to Dennriall, watching Aengus thrash. Nibs scurried to us. She climbed Dennriall hiding beneath his long black hair. A keening wail erupted from Aengus and a response from the other cells echoed in the hallway. I understood, Merlin's spell was gone, now held in the spear at our feet, and Aengus was again a slave to the fae who'd created him.

Aengus was alive, but at the cost of his freedom.

Chapter Twenty-One

"Stay back!" Dennriall ordered when I stood up and took a step toward Aengus. He'd crawled as far as his manacled ankles allowed, snapping his teeth and grasping air trying to grab us.

"What do we do?" The words seared my throat. This wasn't my fault, and yet guilt gnawed at my core. Logic couldn't dispel the ache as I gazed on Aengus devoid of all that had been him.

Dennriall sighed at my question, but didn't answer. From below, Nibs patted my leg. I reached down and pulled her into my arms. Her feather-light weight against my chest was a small comfort, but her unusal silence was not.

The sudden sound of a descending stampede reverberating off the walls startled us. The decibels increased like an oncoming train through a tunnel. We only had time to turn toward the noise, as three *ossorians* burst into the room, bringing the smell of wet dog and rotten meat with them. Snarling, they slid to a stop between Aengus and where we stood, their claws leaving gouges in the stone. Beside me, Dennriall whispered the name *ossorian*, his jeweled eyes wide in disbelief. "It's impossible."

I jerked my head his way in surprise. "What do you mean impossible? This is the third time this has happened to me."

Aengus gave a growl from the floor, his fingers nearly wrapping around the leg of one of the *ossorians*. It kicked at him and stepped farther out of reach.

"The *ossorians* haven't been seen since the veil closed." Dennriall's tone and expression were both furious.

Before I could make the argument that oviously someone sent them, one of the *ossorians* rose up on its back legs and I knew from before it was going to speak. Its muzzle pulled away from its massive jaws and the creature slurred through its long, sharp teeth, "You will come."

Dennriall snapped his fingers and he no longer looked human. His four upper limbs twitched with tension and he set all of them against his torso posing with assertion. "As the Unseelie seneschal, I go only where my queen commands."

"You will come," a second *ossorian* repeated, the one who had kicked out at Aengus. "Unharmed or broken."

Behind the three beasts, Aengus had managed to stand, presenting a better view of his ripped tunic stained with blood. He swayed, arms loose and back hunched. His eyes were still milky and held nothing but need. All intellegence swept away, leaving only a feral beast. I remembered our discussion last night. He'd told me before Merlin's spell he'd needed the blood of the Honeythorn line to stay sane. Somewhere, upstairs were Theo and Aurnia. Could their blood help? Or was it too late?

I pointed at Aengus. "We'll go with you, but not without our friend." The *ossorians* cocked their head in confusion and Dennriall swung his torso around to glare down at me, his tri-jeweled eyes deep red.

Nibs yanked hard on my dress top. "No, too dangerous," she whispered.

I nodded in agreement. "I know, but we don't have a choice." I looked up at Dennriall for confirmation. He sighed deeply, letting his eyes blink closed and opened his arms wide in reluctant agreement. Mostly confident I was making the right stand, I turned my attention to the lead *ossorian.* "He goes or we stay." For a brief second, I contemplated the fact that "old" Genny would never have demanded anything, especially from a fae. But "new" Genny seemed bound and determined to get us killed.

Without a word, the lead *ossorian* gestured for Aengus to be grabbed and the closest one grunted an affirmative. With a yank, the *ossorian* ripped the anchor holding the manacles out of the floor, then it grabbed one of Aengus's arms and jerked him onto its shoulder in a fireman's hold. Aengus howled and thrashed, but the *ossorian* remained unfazed. It lumbered past us out the door and into the hallway.

The lead *ossorian*, bent over and grabbed the spear that had syphoned Merlin's spell from Aengus and stepped out gesturing for us to follow. Dennriall leaned his torso toward me and whispered, "Your debt to me is very large," before he skittered forward. I left the blood soaked fabric I'd used for Nibs on the floor and instead used Aengus's disgarded tartan, the brooch still hanging on. I pinned it secure and set Nibs within the new sling, before I grabbed up Excalibur and walked out, too. The last *ossorian* brought up the rear.

As we made our way through the blue glow toward the stairs, the tormented cries from behind the other doors haunted our ears as we ascended.

I wouldn't have believed it, but I was actually happy to reach the faux dungeon and it's fake sconces after our excursion down into the catacombs. I took a deep cleansing breath, only to choke on "eau du *ossorian*." Nibs held her nose and stuck out her tongue and we both smiled. The tension in my shoulders and chest, eased for a moment and I was grateful.

Then ahead of us, Aengus let out a keening wail and thrashed harder against his captor, who merely adjusted his charge with a shoulder bump and continued on. All my tension returned.

We took a hallway that led us to the large circular foyer with the elevator. A group of fae congregated, including the Unseelie queen and the Seelie ruler. Both no longer dressed in their respective styles, but were robed in deep jewel tones. One of magenta and one of emerald. Gaius and Theo stood near Lady Aurnia and my father — the Green Knight — loomed nearly hunching behind Saoirsa. There were a few I didn't know also among the group and a number of identical trell hovered on the edges.

The fae entourage heard us arrive. My father turned his helmeted head in my direction and gave the barest of nods. So subtle, I almost wasn't sure I saw it. Saoirsa, the Unseelie queen, pointed at the *ossorian* leading us and her eyes widened. She spun toward Lady Aurnia, her finger stabbing into the other leader's magenta robes. "You have broken the treaty!"

Aurnia slapped Saoirsa's finger away. "Those aren't mine!"

Saoirsa huffed in disbelief. "Just like you don't have the *fola tráill* hidden in your basement."

Both snapped their mouths shut as the three *ossorians* drew near, but the beasts did not stop before the fae leaders, instead they made their way to a fae who lingered off to the side. She was a bent old woman, whose hair lay lank and grey and whose skin hung from her bones like wrinkled dough. She smiled motherly at the beasts, then turned her eyes on me and winked.

Aurnia and Saoirsa looked on with questioning faces.

Saoirsa was the first to speak. "These beasts are yours, Mistress Crone?"

The old fae smiled giving full view to her broken and discolored teeth. "An unfortunate necessity in my duty to keep Underhill safe. Without them, we would not have known of Lady Aurnia's near-disastrous plan."

Lady Aurnia glared.

The *ossorian* carrying Aengus, threw him to the floor and Aengus let out another scream, startling everyone. He scrambled, trying to stand, but the manacles on his ankles tripped him and sent him back down to the flagstones. I winced and stopped myself from reaching out to help.

"Theo!" Aurnia bellowed and her son, squeezed out from between Gaius and another fae and dashed to her side. "Feed him," she snapped.

Theo looked down at Aengus and smirked. "Awesome, I see we're back to the way things were."

I stepped forward, Excalibur raised and at the ready. This was the plan. The whole reason, I'd demanded the *ossorians* take Aengus, but now I didn't want Theo anywhere near him. Dennriall rested a limb on my arm and Nibs patted my chest. It was laughable that they thought I was dangerous — but that wasn't true anymore, was it? I noticed then the magic pulsing within me. It pushed against my skin. I found the golden strand that rested in Theo. I longed to reach out and grab hold. Tingles raced down my scalp and gold tinged the edges of my vision. The chaos inside longed to be unfettered and deadly.

I trembled and let my sword tip drop, just like my stomach.

Theo pulled out a dagger from his boot and dug the tip into his wrist and I forced myself to keep watch. If Aengus needed me, I'd be ready. Blood flowed and dripped from the wound. Before Theo could lift the blade away, Aengus howled and leapt. They both tumbled to the floor, the dagger clattering from Theo's hand. Aengus straddled Theo's chest and held Theo's arm to his mouth, sucking on it with relish.

I finally looked away.

This wasn't right. This wasn't the man who'd come to my rescue or even the man who'd sat on the couch watching cheesy teen television. Aengus wasn't a monster. I bit back a sob.

Saoirsa paid the scene no heed and gestured toward the three of us. Nibs levered herself higher out of the sling. "Evil queen who steals clothes!" She shook her fist toward the Unseelie queen, who did not respond.

Saoirsa surveyed me, then looked to Dennriall. "Seneschal, she is not marked?"

Dennriall dipped into a curtsy-like bow, his front legs bending at the knee. "She was unharmed."

"Step forward, mongrel," Saoirsa said hooking a finger toward me.

I glanced at Dennriall, then at Nibs, and I even hesitated a quick glance at Aengus, before dropping my gaze to Excalibur. Three days ago, I was just a museum intern who drove retirement home residents to their appointments, who had no family left, and who avoided the fae like the plague.

Excalibur warmed in my hand and the barest tendrils of my newfound magic eeked out twisting and swirling down my arm and back up again. The weight of the sword in my hand felt right. The magic felt as natural as any physical part of me.

For three days, I had not thought once about my words or how I might look to anyone else. I had been completely myself. No disembling. No hiding.

My life before had been safe and comfortable, but it was a lie. Grandpa had tried to protect me by keeping me sequestered and secret, but I had fae blood — and witch blood. I was a Cailleach fae. Special. And dangerous. I looked hard at both fae leaders.

"I prefer the term *custos*."

Lady Aurnia rolled her eyes. "The Roman title changes nothing."

I ignored her.

Saoirsa glared over at Lady Aurnia. "No, but there is another title she claims that does." Saoirsa turned toward me, her garish makeup giving her a monstrous look in the dungeon's flickering light. "My Green Knight, formerly the witch Geoffrey Corbin, is he or is he not your father?"

"He is," I agreed as I eyed my father. The knight shifted, taking a step closer.

"You nearly marked a Cailleach fae as a *fola tráill*, releasing all that chaotic energy and likely bringing Underhill to ruin!" Saoirsa reprimanded.

Lady Aurnia narrowed her eyes. "They are rare. How was I to know she was one? Besides, that is just speculation. It's never been proven."

"Your desire to control the veil has made you blind. You put us all at risk with your ambition."

Beneath the conversation, the looping tract of the *ossorian's* wet breathing and Aengus lapping at Theo's wrist drew more attention when half of it stopped. Aengus huddled next to the stone wall, blood dripping from his bottom lip, over his chin and down his neck. Theo, unharmed, stood and wrapped a kerchief someone tossed him around his wrist. Then he reached down and grabbed the back of Aengus's tunic, yanking him up roughly to his feet. Aengus's eyes, now golden again, found mine and he looked away in shame, hunching in on himself. "Wait!" I cried out as Theo led him away.

One of the trell stepped forward and stopped me from following.

I clenched Excalibur hard until the joints in my hand popped and ached. Gold rimmed my gaze until only the narrowest channel was not bathed in the glow. I wasn't as close to Underhill as I had been in the catacombs, but every part of me wanted to reach out and devour every bit of magic I could.

I spun the bracelet hoping for my mother to calm me. She didn't come, but I felt Nibs climb to my shoulder and say my name. I couldn't pull my eyes away from the retreating form of Theo and Aengus. "You could become chaos. We could die," Nibs said softly against my ear.

Cailleach fae don't live long, Jane had told me. Some were killed, others burned themselves out, unable to control their magic. Did I really want to be responsible for all their deaths. I shuddered and closed my eyes, heaving large lungfuls of air until I calmed. "Thank you, Nibs." She patted my cheek.

"He is no longer your concern," Lady Aurnia commanded when she noticed my desire to follow Aengus. I nearly growled as I swung toward her. Excalibur raised to attack, gold only just fading from my vision.

"Peace," Mistress Crone hissed over us all and everyone turned her way, silent. With knarled hands, she took the spear from one of the *ossorians* and held it across both palms. "Birgha," she murmured and pinned her gaze on Lady Aurnia. "The spear is turgid with Merlin's magic. How did you plan to pass it to the girl?"

Lady Aurnia dipped a curtsy. "My mage was going to study the spell, Mistress. Find a way to recreate it. With time we would have succeeded." Her words were confident, but her tone sounded weak.

"Hmmm." Mistress Crone pursed her lips. She spun the spear, stopping it with a slap against her open hand. "Then you would control the veil? Opening and closing it according to your whim? Barring passage to those you deem unworthy?"

Lady Aurnia's nod was unsure. She clearly heard the accusation in the old woman's questions. Saoirsa stepped close to Aurnia. "My sister chose poorly, but the veil cannot stay open. You must agree, Goddess?"

Was Mistress Crone a goddess? I had only just accepted my place in the fae world. Would I now need to worry about dieties, too?

"I would speak with your mage." Mistress Crone set the butt of the spear on the ground with a knock, waiting. Lady Aurnia eager to make amends urged Gaius forward. The mage maneuvered his way out in front of the pack and bowed to the old fae woman.

She smiled wide, her mouth dark as a void. She lowered the

spear and stepped close. "Do you honor your goddess?" she asked harshly.

Gaius looked unsettled. "Of course, Mistress Crone."

"Good," she growled and drove the spear into his gut.

The corridor erupted in screams.

Chapter Twenty-Two

"Mistress Crone, why?" Lady Aurnia cried.

The old fae woman tore the spear from Gaius, who let out a startled yelp and fell to his knees gasping, his eyes bulging beneath his raised eyebrows as blood, dark and thick, escaped through his fingers holding his abdomen. She stood over the mage, the silver spear tip dripping red. With a flick of her fingers, just as Dennriall had demonstrated in the catacombs below, she dropped the crone glamour. All now saw her gleaming like a white star in the the dungeon gloom — the Lady in White.

"Leannan Sidhe!" Saoirsa stumbled back, pulling Lady Aurnia with her. Both of them called their warriors to attend them and four trell and the Green Knight rushed forward, massive axe primed to swing.

"Murderer." The Brownie's words dripped with disgust.

I remembered that name from the diner. Leannan Sidhe had been Danu's consort, the fae who'd been the gatekeeper of the veil and after he went missing she led the uprising. She was the reason the veil was closed completely.

It seemed the Lady in White and the Leannan Sidhe, were the

same. She'd helped when the Seelie court had tried to mark me, but was she actually the villain? Gaius dead on the floor, a trail of blood dripping from his slack mouth, seemed like hard evidence. I hadn't trusted him, but I hadn't wanted him dead.

Leannan smiled as she ran a hand over the spear, then she held it out before her. "All I needed was a little blood sacrifice and Merlin's magic." Her eyes rolled back until not even her pale irises could be seen. The air around the spear shimmered then pulsed with a shock wave that disappeared into her body. Her eyes flickered forward and she smiled one side raised high enough to see sharp teeth. "It's tempting to monologue, but now that I'm no longer trapped. I think I'll take my leave." She circled her hand in the air toward the dungeon wall. A portion, large enough for two people to walk abreast appeared to fall inward, revealing a swirling mist beyond. Prisms of color undulated within like a living being.

"Grab her, boys," Leannan called to the *ossorians*, pointing directly at me.

"Stop her!" Lady Aurnia and Saoirsa cried simultaneously Leannan stepped toward the portal. The trell pulled bronze short swords from hidden sheaths and stalked forward in formation.

The three beasts ignored the trell and lumbered toward me. I raised Excalibur, hoping to defend myself without setting off the time bomb of magic within me. Bombs caused casualties, but gold still flickered at the corner of my sight.

Certainly the Unseelie queen had meant for Dennriall to obey her command, he was her seneschal after all, instead he stayed close to my side. And the Green Knight, my father, did not go after Leannan either. He turned his helmet of verdure my way. With a lunge he plunged between the oncoming *ossorians* and me, his axe swinging in massive arches. His tread like mini earthquakes.

Everything around me stretched into moments, slowing even as my mind sped up.

The beasts dug their nails into the stone as they lunged. One *ossorian* ducked beneath the Green Knight's falling axe blade and ran up the foliage along his back. With a snarl it sank it's teeth into the knight's vine covered shoulder. He reached up and ripped the beast away with a roar. With a heave, he sent the *ossorian* sailing through the portal.

The trell tried to reach Leannan, but with a snap of her finger she sent them crashing to the floor. Unconcious? Dead? I couldn't tell. Nibs squeaked in her sling, her head peaking over her hands clutching the fabric.

Dennriall stepped in the way of another *ossorian* trying to make its way to me. He kicked out from one side, connecting with the beast, sending it rolling to the Green Knight who while defending himself from the last *ossorian*, managed to grab the incoming beast and punt it into the mist and away.

Leannan called her last *ossorian* to her. As it scrambled to obey, its jaws snapped in a frenzy, latching onto one of Dennriall's legs. Before any of us could reach out to stop it, both Dennriall and the last ossorian were engulfed by the portal.

"No!" I yelled and the Unseelie queen cried out with me.

The Green Knight's plate-sized hand landed heavy on my shoulder and I realized I'd moved to follow.

The Lady in White, Leannan's eyes found mine. "I will have that power," she threatened. Her stare held me hostage as the cold knowledge of her true motivation left me frozen. She hadn't wanted Gaius to mark me, not to save me, but to keep my power safe — for her. She was the fae Jane had warned of, those that killed the Cailleach fae for their chaotic magic. Leannan finally turned away and slipped into the mist, the portal snapping shut behind them. She was gone.

So was Dennriall.

Nobody moved. Nobody spoke. As if we were all turned to stone.

Lady Aurnia was first to shake the torpor. She made her way in silence over to Gaius. The edge of her magenta robe darkened with blood from the pool beneath the dead mage. The trell that had fallen at Leannan's feet began to stir, but Lady Aurnia did not appear pleased. She lifted the hem of her robe from the blood and stepped back, looking in my direction.

"You must see now how important it is to close the veil?" Her words implied I'd somehow helped to create the disaster around her.

She could take her gaslighting and shove it. None of this was my fault. Aengus was suffering because of her. Dennriall was gone now, too. She might not be the villain in this scenario, but she certainly wasn't the hero. The Green Knight's — my father's — gentle, but heavy grip over my shoulder was the only thing that kept me from yelling all my thoughts at her, which would probably have set off the barely controlled magic inside me.

Saoirse spoke up. "We all must work together, or we will all falter under Leannan's guile"

"That was your goddess, not mine." I crossed my arms.

Both Aurnia and Saoirsa looked uncomfortable, but it was Saoirsa who explained. "We were misled. Mistress Crone, Fódla, was not among us. Leannan is not a goddess. She is a traitor to our people."

Aurnia pointed a finger at me. "We'll need Excalibur, we'll need *you*, to fix this."

I ducked out from under my father's hand and raised Excalibur toward them. "Are you going to fix Aengus? Are you going to save Dennriall? And my father?" I pointed at the Green Knight behind me. I wondered about my mother, too, but I feared they'd confirm she was dead if I asked and that would mean I'd talked with her ghost. I wasn't ready to accept that yet. "Because honestly that's all I care about at this point. You and your courts have caused nothing but harm."

From her sling, Nibs added a, "Fix the bad," for good measure.

Aurnia cocked her head. "I'm sure deals can be arranged."

"No deals!" Gold instantly swam in my vision and I took a deep, calming breath.

Both fae women took a step back. They were well aware of what a Cailleach fae could do. What I could do. Calmer now, I repeated. "No deals. You will save my friends and family and then I'll consider helping close the veil."

Saoirsa huffed. "Your father made his choice. It cannot be broken until another challenges him. If he dies the other will become my Green Knight."

"Find a way," I said, not accepting her answer.

I turned toward the direction I thought was the elevator.

"You can't leave," Saoirsa stepped into my path. "We need Excalibur, we must find out how it has been altered, why it chose you."

"I'm going home." Leannan would be back and the only place she couldn't reach me was behind the wards my grandfather and the witches had created. I wanted to save Dennriall and Aengus, but I couldn't if I was dead. I glared at the Unseelie queen. "Unless you think you can stop me?"

Saoirsa paled.

The Green Knight's harsh whisper silenced us all. "The sword in the stone." I furrowed my brow, not understanding. He mimed driving a sword downward with the handle of his axe.

Oh! A perfect solution. I lifted Nibs out of the sling and placed her on her feet. "I'll meet you by the elevator," I told her and the Brownie smiled wide and scurried off. I wasn't sure how much magic I'd need to accomplish it, but I didn't want her close just in case. I raised Excalibur, blade tip pointed down. I closed my eyes, imagined the sword sinking into the stone below me, and let my consciousness fall as the tendrils of gold twisted upward and exploded behind my eyes as the sword tip hit the floor.

I looked around. No one seemed harmed and Excalibur stood, half embedded in the flagstone at my feet. I grinned. Maybe I was getting the hang of this magic thing. "Here, I'll leave the sword with you." An idea popped into my mind and a I ran with it. "And the Green Knight will come home with me so I'm protected." My father gave a slow nod in agreement, the leaves of his armor rustling.

Saoirsa sighed and Aurnia waved her hand in irritated aquiencence. I gave an awkward bow. It didn't hurt to be nice when you're getting your way. My father waded through what was left of the fae group and they parted to give him room. I followed after him.

Had I really just bested both fae courts? I'd better get home behind the wards before they realized it was just luck.

Chapter Twenty-Three

The walk home in my slashed and bloody dress, Aengus's tartan draped over my shoulder and my Doc Martins clomping loudly on the sidewalk, raised eyebrows even without them being able to see the massive wall of plant life — the Green Knight — that followed me. Or the Brownie who perched on my shoulder chatting at him. I think Nibs meant to tell my father a summary of her year with me, but what she talked about was mostly clothes and food.

The looks didn't bother me as much as they had in the past. Sure, to the residents of Carson City I was weird, and my outfit proved it, but to myself I now lived in far more dimensions than just the one they'd put me in.

As I walked, I found myself clenching and unclenching my right hand — already missing the weight of Excalibur. But the loss of the sword didn't sit as heavy as my thoughts of Aengus and Dennriall. I spun the bracelet on my wrist and glanced over my shoulder at my father. I'd find a way to save them all.

The Green Knight found a spot in the front yard of the retirement home and literally planted his feet. Vines sank deep below the topsoil and he set his axe upon his shoulder to wait as Nibs and I made our way inside.

All the lights were on, but it didn't vanquish the oppressive pall that filled the house. Something was wrong.

Everett appeared from the hallway. He rushed forward in relief, his large frame feeling smaller after all my time with the Green Knight. "Girl, I've been calling you. Where have you been?"

I couldn't explain, not quickly, so I just asked, "What happened?" Everett didn't answer as his eyes moved from me to my shoulder, and I realized Nibs had decided to drop her glamour.

"I really do promise we'll have that talk, but I need you to tell me what happened," I said firmly and Everett seemed to snap out it.

"It's Ms. Carlson, she collapsed after you ran off. The residents won't let me anywhere near her until they speak with you."

Something was wrong with Jane? I grabbed Nibs and held her out to Everett. He automatically put out his hands, but his eyes widened when I plopped her into them. Then I dashed up the main staircase as Everett called after me. "I'm a nurse. There are protocols. No one's going to believe me when I tell them a bunch of over eighties kept me out of a damn room."

In the hallway in front of Jane's bedroom, three of the residents stood hand-in-hand, head bowed. The air shimmered around them, heaviest in front of the open doorway.

"I'm here," I called as I ran to them. Mr. Friedman dropped Mr. Perez and Mrs. Liu's hands and turned, pushing his glasses back up onto his nose. "We've taken turns all night holding her here. She needed to speak with you. About your magic. It's free, isn't it?" I nodded and Mr. Friedman gave an accepting shrug. "Go in, she's waiting."

The room felt cold, the kind of cold that settles deep in the bones and stays. Jane lay on the bed and I knew she was dead. All the life had left her and now she was as inert as the mattress she lay on. Only an object, no longer a being.

"Took you long enough," Jane chastised from the window seat.

The weak afternoon sun shown through her, emphasizing her translucent state. And now I understood what Mr. Friedman meant when he said they'd been holding her here. "I'm sorry," I whispered.

"You'd better be sorry for wasting my time and not for me dying." When I opened my mouth to speak, she hushed me. "We don't have much time. Story of our lives, huh? But you've got magic now, felt it the moment my spell fell, and now I won't be here to help you. The coven can try, but even together they aren't strong enough to even reset the wards. It's mostly my residual magic keeping me here. You'll need to learn fast and that means keeping your man out of the house until you can manage on your own." She winked in jest, but noticed immediately when I couldn't join her.

I rolled my lips, fighting the tears. "The fae took Merlin's spell. Aengus is their prisoner now." The weight of the truth for a moment felt too hard to bear and I wanted to slip to the floor. Inside I could feel my magic twist in on itself, hiding from the hurt.

Jane harumphed. "Well, looks like you'll need to learn even faster so you can recast it."

Shock straightened me. "Recast Merlin's spell?"

"Why not, he was no more powerful than you."

"Are you saying that Merlin was a Cailleach fae? But you said they didn't live long."

"I said most. Most is not all, and yes, that's exactly what I'm saying."

The gold tendrils uncoiled slightly, my grief giving way to a slim touch of hope.

Jane turned toward the window. "Reach out to other covens. Find someone strong enough to teach you. Now, I'm off to find my Mary." Her face screwed up in confusion as she looked down on the lawn. "Is that a topiary in the front yard?"

A startled laugh escaped me. "It's kind of my dad."

"Gives new meaning to the term 'family tree', doesn't it?" she teased with a wink and took a step toward the light.

"Wait!" I reached out a hand as if to stop her.

Jane paused, but only barely. "I've got places to be, spit it out."

"Ghosts, ghosts that stay in this realm I mean, they're connected to a place or an item." Jane nodded. I lifted my wrist and showed the bracelet. "I've seen my mom with this on, but she doesn't stay and it's like she gets pulled away."

"Doesn't sound like a ghost. That sounds like she's using that bracelet as a conduit to speak from wherever she is. You're going to have to find out where that is. I'm sorry I can't be here to help."

I smiled and clutched my wrist with the bracelet to my chest. "No, it's okay. You need to go to Mary."

"Your grandfather would be proud," Jane said, her voice unusually gentle.

I shook my head. "But I'm doing everything he told me not to." The words didn't fill me with guilt. I no longer doubted my choices and I'd make them again. But Grandpa had tried to keep me safe and I realized I might never be safe again and I would never have the chance to explain to him why.

"No, you aren't following his path. You're following yours, which means you don't need to be safe anymore. You need to be free. And that would make him very proud."

I smiled at Jane through a watery haze and she smiled back. She turned and walked toward the window, losing more and more of her diaphonous form until she was barely a wisp of a body. And then she disappeared completely.

I swiped my palms across my cheeks, trying to rub away the tears and crawled up onto the window seat. Below, in the last golden vestiges of the afternoon stood the Green Knight, unmoving. I might no longer be hidden and safe, but I was protected. I spun the bracelet connecting me to my mother and I could almost hear her voice. I wouldn't have made it home without her or Dennriall. For a moment, my chest ached over the memory of him being dragged into the portal. Would the Leannan Sidhe kill him? Was death the worst that could happen?

Aengus.

It should have been the memory of when I stepped out of the bathroom in the dress that was now rags and he'd called me "enchanting" that held the place of honor in my mind. But it wasn't. It was the moment in the diner when he'd known how scared I was, and without hesitation, had slid to the back of the booth so I would not be caged in.

I thought of the cells in the catacombs. Was Aengus caged there now? Or was he somewhere else? With someone else? At the thought of Aurnia or Theo laying their hands on Aengus all grief burned away. So far from the courts and Excalibur, I found my connection to the magic somewhat muted, but even still I fought the urge to drown in it. Jane was right. I needed to find a teacher. And fast. I stood up from the window, wiping the last of the salt trails from my face.

Mr. Friedman and the rest of the residents peered into the room, worry etched in their craggy faces. I squared my shoulders.

"Let's get started."

The story continues in *The Hidden Druid*
Available now

Visit Angela's website for updates!

Pronunciation Guide for the Innisfail Cycle

Aengus – pronounced like Angus

Angusulus – an-G (soft g)US-ah-luhs

Cailleach – Coll-yoch

Cathal – Cah - hall

Cynosure – Sy-na-shoor

Geoffrey – pronounced like Jeffrey

Leannan Sidhe – Lee-AHN-nahn Shee

Saoirse – SUR -sha

Aurnia – OR-neeah

Theophilus – THEE-ah-phi-luhs

Gaius – GUY-uhs

Dennriall – DEN – Ree – all

Innisfail – IN -nis – fail

Ossorians – OH – sore – ree- ans

Fola Traill – FOH – lah TRAY – all

Sul Aos Si – Sool – Ees – she

Tá mo chroí istigh ionat -- Taw mu kree iss-chig uhn-it

Aodh – A (long a sound)

Uisce – ish-cah

More ways to stay in touch with Angela Laverghetta

Thank you so much for picking up The Hidden Druid. If you enjoyed it, please consider leaving a review. Indie authors rely on reviews and your honest words will help the right readers find it.

If you'd like to get updates on future books you can join my newsletter by going to my website:

www.angelalaverghettabooks.com

You can also follow me on social media—

Instagram, Threads, and TikTok: @angelawithapen

Facebook: Angela Laverghetta

Angela Laverghetta

Angela Laverghetta is a Northern Nevada based fantasy author. She's taken the saying "write what you know" to heart and loves showing readers a different side of Nevada. Almost all her writings take place locally, including her debut modern fantasy novel The Buried Knight published in 2023, and its sequel The Hidden Druid. Other published works include a novella previously published by a small press and two short stories both for The ACES Anthology in 2023 and 2024. When not writing, you can find her handling her zoo of many pets, talking to her youngest son about comics and fanfiction, or curling up in a blanket with a mug of tea and a stack of four or five books in easy reach.

Through it all she found comfort and (more importantly) escape in reading and writing. Her goal as an author is to provide the same comfort and escape for her readers.